Coming Home for Christmas: Three Holiday Stories

Enduring Light

Marriage of Mercy

My Loving Vigil Keeping

Her Hesitant Heart

The Double Cross

Safe Passage

Carla Kelly's Christmas Collection

In Love and War

A Timeless Romance Anthology: Old West Collection

Marco and the Devil's Bargain

Softly Falling

Paloma and the Horse Traders

Reforming Lord Ragsdale

Enduring Light

Summer Campaign

Doing No Harm

Nonfiction

*On the Upper Missouri: The Journal
of Rudolph Friedrich Kurz*

Fort Buford: Sentinel at the Confluence

Stop Me If You've Read This One

FOR THIS
WE ARE
Soldiers

TALES OF THE FRONTIER ARMY

FOR THIS
WE ARE
Soldiers
TALES OF THE FRONTIER ARMY

CARLA
KELLY

SWEETWATER
BOOKS
An imprint of Cedar Fort, Inc.
Springville, Utah

"A Season for Heroes," "Mary Murphy," and "Such Brave Men" originally appeared in *Here's to the Ladies: Stories of the Frontier Army*, published by Texas Christian University, 2004. "Break a Leg" originally appeared in *A Timeless Romance Anthology: The Western Collection*, Mirror Press, 2014.

ISBN 13: 978-1-4621-1924-0

Published by Sweetwater Books, an imprint of Cedar Fort, Inc.
2373 W. 700 S., Springville, UT 84663
Distributed by Cedar Fort, Inc., www.cedarfort.com

LIBRARY OF CONGRESS CATALOGING-IN-PUBLICATION DATA

Names: Kelly, Carla, author.
Title: For this we are soldiers / Carla Kelly.
Description: Springville, Utah : Sweetwater Books, an imprint of Cedar Fort, Inc., [2016]
Identifiers: LCCN 2016028874 (print) | LCCN 2016033464 (ebook) | ISBN 9781462119240 (perfect bound : alk. paper) | ISBN 9781462127047 (epub, pdf, mobi)
Subjects: LCSH: Nineteenth century, setting. | West (U.S.), setting. | LCGFT: Short stories. | Historical fiction. | Western fiction. | War fiction.
Classification: LCC PS3561.E3928 F67 2016 (print) | LCC PS3561.E3928 (ebook) | DDC 813/.54--dc23
LC record available at https://lccn.loc.gov/2016028874

Cover design by Rebecca Greenwood
Cover design © 2016 by Cedar Fort, Inc.
Edited and typeset by Jessica Romrell

Printed in the United States of America

10 9 8 7 6 5 4 3 2 1

Printed on acid-free paper

To Susan Porter, who is every bit as courageous as these nineteenth-century ladies, and to Rita Schofield, a traveling buddy who helped me with a plot point. Thanks, friends!

Contents

Introduction

I need to explain this title. The historian in me won't let me rest until I do.

In graduate school in Louisiana, I studied American history with the emphasis on the Indian Wars (1854–1890). We were a raucous bunch, and opinionated, but ultimately more skeptical than anything else, as good historians should be.

I am not sure in which discussion or class this happened, but when one of us would say something attributed to a historical figure, but not likely the actual fact, someone would say, "He didn't really say that." Everyone else would chorus, "But he should have!"

1

So it is with "For this we are soldiers." Supposedly this was said by Captain Guy V. Henry, D Company, Third Cavalry, after he was terribly wounded in the face during the Battle of the Rosebud, Montana Territory, June 17, 1876.

I spent some useful time studying Guy Henry, who was awarded a Medal of Honor for his role in the Battle of Cold Harbor during the Civil War, served with distinction through a long career in the West, fought in Puerto Rico in the Spanish American War, and served briefly as governor of Puerto Rico.

At the Rosebud, he was shot through the face and knocked off his horse in the middle of a ferocious battle. The bullet entered under his left eye, shattered his cheekbone, blew out some teeth, and came out just under his right eye.

His life was saved by Shoshone Indian allies who fought the Lakota literally over his body. Later, he was hauled to the first aid station and lay there for a few more hours, with no protection from the sun except his horse's shadow. In a hard-drinking, betting army, no one would have wagered a dime on Henry's life expectancy.

As the story goes, once the battle ended, Guy Henry's fellow officers came by to inquire how he was. This is where Henry said, "It is nothing. For this we are soldiers."

Ah, but historians are skeptical. It's a matter of some dispute that Henry could have said anything of the kind, considering the nature of his facial wounds. Many Indian Wars historians, me included, think he probably said nothing at all. This is where we reply, "But he should have!"

And so Captain Henry should have. It still remains, true or not, one of the better quotations about any soldier in any war, strained to the utmost and soldiering on. The historian in me would never allow anyone to think he really said it, but by golly, what a statement! The fiction writer in me couldn't waste it.

This anthology of Indian Wars short stories before you mainly describes another kind of warrior in the Indian Wars—the women and children who followed their husbands and fathers out onto the plains after the Civil War and in many cases spent their entire lives in isolated garrisons from the Mississippi River to the Pacific Coast.

The army never officially recognized the wives of officers, non-commissioned officers and enlisted men, calling them mere "camp followers." These army dependents fought their own war against fear and disease and death, and they were no less brave than the men.

"A Season for Heroes," "Mary Murphy," and "Such Brave Men," are also found in my collection, *Here's to the Ladies: Stories of the Frontier,* published by Texas Christian University in 2004, and used here with grateful permission. "Break a Leg" came from *A Timeless Romance Anthology: Old West Collection* (Mirror Press, 2014). The remaining stories I wrote especially for this anthology.

And to those of you who have waited for a whole new novel from me, wait a bit longer, please. On November 9, 2015, and January 25, 2016, I had total knee replacements, which put me way behind my writing schedule. This little collection will hopefully fill the gap until I can deliver another novel in 2017.

People sometimes ask me what my personal favorite books are. My Indian Wars short stories occupy that position, partly because of my love for the subject, and partly because of the wonderful rangers and historians that I met while working at Fort Laramie National Historic Site and Fort Union Trading Post National Historic Site. These colleagues remain my dear friends.

For this we are writers.

Carla Kelly

Such Brave Men

"A little paint will make all the difference," Hart Sanders said as he and his wife surveyed the scabby walls in Quarters B.

Emma stood on tiptoe to whisper in her husband's ear. She didn't want to offend the quartermaster sergeant, who was leaning against the door and listening (she was sure). "Hart, what are these walls made of?"

"Adobe," he whispered back.

"Oh." Perhaps she could find out what adobe was later.

Hart turned to the sergeant in the doorway. The man straightened up when the lieutenant spoke to him. "Sergeant, have some men bring our household effects here. And we'll need a bed, table, and chairs from supply."

"Yes, sir."

Emma took off her bonnet and watched the sergeant heading back to the quartermaster storehouse. Then she turned and looked at her first army home again. Two rooms and a lean-to kitchen, the allotment of a second lieutenant.

Hart was watching her. Theirs wasn't a marriage of long standing, but she knew him well enough to know that he wanted to smile but wasn't sure how she would take that. "Not exactly Sandusky, is it?" he ventured finally.

She grinned at him and snapped his suspenders. "It's not even Omaha, Hart, and you know it!"

But I have been prepared for this, she thought to herself later as she blacked the cook stove in the lean-to. Hart had warned her about life at Fort Laramie, Dakota Territory. He had told her about the wind and the heat and the cold and the bugs and the dirt. But sitting in the parlor of her father's house in Sandusky, she hadn't dreamed of anything quite like this.

Later that afternoon, as she was tacking down an army blanket for the front room carpet, she noticed that the ceiling was shedding. Every time she hammered in a tack, white flakes drifted down to the floor and settled on her hair, the folding rocking chair, and the whatnot shelf she had carried on her lap from Cheyenne Depot to Fort Laramie. She swept out the flakes after the blanket was secure and reminded herself to step lightly in the front room.

Dinner was brought in by some of the other officers' wives, and they dined on sowbelly, hash browns, and eggless custard. The sowbelly looked definitely lowbrow congealing on her Lowestoft bridal china, and she wished she had brought along tin plates like Hart had suggested.

She was putting the last knickknack on the whatnot when Hart got into bed in the next room. The crackling and rustling startled her, and she nearly dropped the figurine in her hand. She hurried to the door. "Hart? Are you all right?" she asked.

He had blown out the candle, and the bedroom was dark. "Well, sure, Emma. What's the matter?"

"That awful noise!"

She heard the rustling again as he sat up in bed. "Emma, haven't you ever slept on a straw-tick mattress?"

"In my father's house?" She shook her head. "Does it ever quiet down?"

"After you sleep on it awhile," he assured her, and the noise started up again as he lay down and rolled over. He laughed. "Well, my dear, be grateful that we're not in a connecting duplex. This bed's not really discreet, is it?"

She felt her face go red, then laughed too, and put down the figurine.

She had finished setting the little house in order the next morning when Hart came bursting into the front room. He waved a piece of paper in front of her nose.

"Guess what?" he shouted. "D Company is going on detached duty to Fetterman! We leave tomorrow!"

"Do I get to come?" she asked.

"Oh, no. We'll be gone a couple of months. Isn't it exciting? My first campaign!"

Well, it probably was exciting, she thought, after he left, but that meant she would have to face the house alone. The prospect gleamed less brightly than it had the night before.

D Company left the fort the next morning after Guard Mount. She was just fluffing up the pillows on their noisy bed when someone knocked on the front door.

It was the adjutant. He took off his hat and stepped into the front room, looking for all the world like a man with bad news. She wondered what could possibly be worse than seeing your husband of one month ride out toward Fetterman—wherever that was—and having to figure out how to turn that scabrous adobe box into a house, let alone a home.

"I hate to tell you this, Mrs. Sanders," he said at last.

"Tell me what?"

"You've been ranked."

Emma shook her head. Whatever was he talking about? Ranked?

"I don't understand, Lieutenant."

He took a step toward her, but he was careful to stay near the door. "Well, you know, ma'am, ranked. Bumped. Bricks falling?"

She stared at him and wondered why he couldn't make sense. Didn't they teach them English at the academy? "I'm afraid it's still a mystery to me, Lieutenant."

He rubbed his hand over his head and shifted from one foot to the other. "You'll have to move, ma'am."

"But I just did," she protested, at the same time surprised at herself for springing to the defense of such a defenseless house.

"I mean again," the lieutenant persisted. "Another lieutenant just reported on post with his wife, and he outranks your husband. Yours is the only quarters available, so you'll have to move."

It took a minute to sink in. "Who? I can't . . ."

She was interrupted by the sound of boots on the front porch. The man who stepped inside was familiar to her, but she couldn't quite place him until he greeted her; then she knew she would never forget that squeaky voice. He was Hart's old roommate from the academy, and she had met him once. She remembered that Hart had told her how the man spent all his time studying and never was any fun at all.

"Are *you* taking my house?" she accused the lieutenant.

"I'm sorry, Mrs. Sanders," he said, but he didn't sound sorry at all.

"But . . . but . . . didn't you just graduate with my husband two months ago? How can you out-rank him?" she asked, wanting to throw both of the officers out of her home.

He smiled again, and she resisted the urge to scrape her fingernails along his face. Instead, she stamped her foot, and white flakes from the ceiling floated down.

"Yes, ma'am, we graduated together, but Hart was forty-sixth in class standing. I was fif-teenth. I still outrank him."

As she slammed the pots and pans into a box and yanked the sheets off the bed, she wished for the first time that Hart had been a little more diligent in his studies.

Two privates moved her into quarters that looked suspiciously like a chicken coop. She sniffed the air in the one-room shack and almost asked one of the privates if the former tenants she ranked out had clucked and laid eggs. But he didn't speak much English, and she didn't feel like wasting her sarcasm.

Emma swept out the room with a vigor that made her cough, and by nightfall when she crawled into the rustling bed, she speculated on the cost of rail fare from Cheyenne to Sandusky.

The situation looked better by morning. The room was small, to be sure, but she was the only one using it, and if she cut up a sheet, curtains would make all the difference. She hung up the Currier and Ives lithograph of sugaring off in Vermont and was ripping up the sheet when someone knocked at the door.

It was the adjutant again. He had to duck to get into the room, and when he straightened up, his head just brushed the ceiling. "Mrs. Sanders," he began, and it was an effort. "I hope you'll understand what I have to tell you."

Emma sensed what was coming and braced herself, but she didn't want to make it easy on him. "What?" she asked, seating herself in the rocking chair and folding her hands in her lap. As she waited for him to speak, she remembered a poem she had read in school called "Horatio at the Bridge."

"You've been ranked out again."

She was silent, looking at him for several moments. She noticed the drops of perspiration gathering on his forehead and that his Adam's apple bobbed up and down when he swallowed.

"And where do I go from here?" she asked at last.

He shuffled his feet and rubbed his head again, gestures she was beginning to recognize. "All we have is a tent, ma'am."

"A tent," she repeated.

"Yes, ma'am."

At least I didn't get attached to my chicken coop, she thought, as she rolled up her bedding. She felt a certain satisfaction in the knowledge that Hart's roommate and his wife—probably a little snip—had been bumped down to her coop by whoever it was that outranked him. "Serves him right," she said out loud as she carried out the whatnot and closed the door.

The same privates set up the tent at the corner of Officers Row. It wasn't even an officer's tent. Because of the increased activity in the field this summer, only a sergeant's tent could be found. The bedstead wouldn't fit in, so the private dumped the bed sack on the grass and put the frame back in the wagon. She started to protest when they drove away, but remembering his shortage of useful English, she saved her breath. They came back soon with a cot.

She had crammed in her trunks, spread the army blanket on the grass, and was setting up the rocking chair when someone rapped on the tent pole.

She knew it would be the adjutant even before she turned around. Emma pulled back the flap and stepped outside. "You can't have it, Lieutenant."

He shook his head and smiled this time. "Oh, no, ma'am. I wasn't going to bump you again." He held out a large square of green fabric.

She took it. "What's this for?"

"Ma'am, I used to serve in Arizona Territory, and most folks down there line tent ceilings with green. Easier on the eyes."

He smiled again, and Emma began to see that the lot of an adjutant was not to be envied. She smiled back.

"Thank you, Lieutenant. I appreciate it." He helped her fasten up the green baize, and it did make a difference inside the tent. Before he left, he pulled her cot away from the tent wall. "So the tent won't leak when it rains," he explained and then laughed. "But it never rains here anyway."

Since she couldn't cook in the tent, she messed with the officers in Old Bedlam that night. There were only three. The adjutant was a bachelor, Captain Endicott was an orphan who had left his family back in the States, and the other lieutenant was casually at post on his way from Fort Robinson to Fort D.A. Russell.

The salt pork looked more at home on a tin plate, and she discovered that plum duff was edible. The coffee burned its way down, but she knew she could get used to it.

She excused herself, ran back to her tent, and returned with the tin of peaches she had bought at the post trader's store for the exorbitant sum of $2.25. The adjutant pried open the lid, and the four of them speared slices out of the can and laughed and talked until Tattoo.

Captain Endicott walked her back to her tent before last call. He shook his head when he saw the tent. "Women ought to stay in the States. Good schools there, doctors, sociability. Much better."

"Don't you miss your family?" she asked.

"Oh, mercy, if you only knew . . . ," he began and then stopped. "Beg pardon, Mrs. Sanders."

He said good night to her and walked off alone to his room in Old Bedlam.

Emma undressed, did up her hair, and got into bed. She lay still, listening to the bugler blow Extinguish Lights. She heard horses snuffling in the officers' stables behind Old Bedlam. When the coyotes started tuning up on the slopes rimming the fort, she pulled the blanket over her head and closed her eyes.

She knew she was not alone when she woke up before Reveille next morning. She sat up and gasped. A snake was curled at the foot of her blanket. She carefully pulled her feet up until she sat in a ball on her pillow. She was afraid to scream because she didn't know what the snake would do, and, besides, she didn't want the sergeant at arms to rush in and catch her with her hair done up in rags.

As she watched and held her breath, the snake unwound itself and moved off the cot. She couldn't see any rattles on its tail, and she slowly let out her breath. The snake undulated across the grass, and she stared at it, fascinated. She hadn't known a reptile could be so graceful. "How do they do that?" she asked herself, as the snake slithered through the grass at the edge of the tent. "I must remember to ask Hart."

She took the rag twists from her hair, pulled on her wrapper, and poked her head out of the tent. The sun was just coming up, and the buildings were tinted with the most delicious shade of pink. She marveled that she could ever have thought the old place ugly.

Her first letter from Hart was handed to her three days later at mail call. She ripped open the envelope and drew out a long, narrow sheet. She read as she walked along the edge of the parade ground.

Dearest Emma,

Pardon this stationery, but I forgot to take any along, and this works better for letters than in the sink (um, that would be a privy to you). Good news. We're going to be garrisoned here permanently, so you'll be moving quite soon, perhaps within the next few days. Or it could be a month. That's the Army. Bad news. Brace yourself. There aren't any quarters available, so we'll have to make do in a tent.

Emma stood still and laughed out loud. A soldier with a large "P" painted on the back of his shirt stopped spearing trash and looked at her, but she didn't acknowledge him. She read on.

It won't be that bad. The commanding officer swears there will be quarters ready by winter. Am looking forward to seeing you soon. I can't express how much I miss you.

Love, Hart

She was almost back to her tent when the adjutant caught up with her.

"Mrs. Sanders," he began. His Adam's apple bobbed, and he put up his hand to rub his head, she was sure.

"It's all right, Lieutenant," she broke in before he could continue. "I've already heard. When am I leaving?"

"In the morning, ma'am."

"I'll be ready."

As she was repacking her trunks that evening, she remembered something her mother had said to her when she left on the train to join Hart in Cheyenne. Mother had dabbed at her eyes and said over and over, "Such brave men, Emma, such brave men!"

Emma smiled.

Break a Leg

Before the story begins

$\mathcal{B}$y August of 1882, Hospital Steward Colm Callahan, 34, had decided he was bored with army life. Perhaps it was just life at Fort Laramie, which used to be interesting during the Great Sioux War. That conflict had ended when most of the hostiles were trundled onto reservations. Someone had definitely waved a white flag and declared the war done when Sitting Bull and his ragged band left Canada and surrendered at Fort Buford in 1881.

The end of the Indian Wars had turned the grand dame of the plains into a backwater garrison. Arrow wounds and amputations had given way to catarrh with copious phlegm (hacks and coughs to laymen), and the occasional case of diarrhea—neither ever interesting. Women of the garrison still gave birth, but the post surgeon managed without help from his hospital steward. Even social diseases had slowed down, to the relief of the surgeon.

On the average morning now, Colm handled sick call with little or no interference from his post surgeon, Captain Dilworth. After nineteen years of army medicine, Colm knew when something warranted the more specialized attention of the post surgeon and in those cases, he summoned the surgeon from the breakfast table accordingly. When it was just catarrh or the dry heaves, he left Captain Dilworth to his newspaper and toast.

Handling sick call meant admonishing any malingerers trying to put one over on the Medical Department, physicking those who needed it and sending them back to the barracks for rest, or hospitalizing the promising few. His reports were done by 10 a.m. and left, squared away, on Captain Dilworth's desk.

Then what? A steward could only count linens, roll bandages, and inventory the pharmacy so often. There was seldom anyone stiff and cold in the dead house to embalm. Lately, Colm found himself upstairs, staring out the window. Situated on a bluff, the hospital commanded a view of the whole garrison.

Depending on his mood, he would look in the direction of the iron bridge—out of his sight—which still saw traffic to the Black Hills, even though the major gold strikes were ancient history now. The Shy-Dead Road, the storied route from Cheyenne to Deadwood, was traveled mostly by law-abiders now. Worse still, rumor hinted that soon the cavalry would be withdrawn, leaving Fort Laramie with infantry only. Colm could almost hear the death knell of the Queen of the Plains.

More profitably, Colm might look out the windows that faced the parade ground. He watched children walking to school, which was held in the newly completed admin building by the Laramie River. Soon mothers with prams would stroll the wooden boardwalks, chatting with one another. That domestic sight sometimes sent him into melancholy, as he remembered desperate days in 1876 and '77, when troops came and went, and war waged all around. Fort

Laramie looked as gentrified as a Midwestern town now. Great Gadfreys and all the Saints!

If Colm was lucky, he might catch a glimpse of Ozzie Washington, easily the prettiest woman on the post, or so he reckoned. Depending on who might be ill among the officers' wives, the lieutenant colonel's wife was kindly inclined to send Ozzie, her servant, with a tureen of nourishing broth, or a loaf or two of bread to the House of Affliction.

Ozzie was not a time waster. Bowl- or basket-laden, she moved at a clip that set her hips swaying so nicely. She was grace personified, moving rapidly but with the dignity of her race. Once—perhaps on a dare from one of the lieutenant colonel's children—Ozzie had set a bushel basket square on her head and wore it the length of Officers Row without mishap. During Reconstruction days in Louisiana, he had seen women of color carry goods that way. So much grace and symmetry had impressed him then and did so now with Ozzie.

Always the observer, he had noticed how nicely the races had mingled for at least a century in New Orleans, producing graceful women of café au lait skin called *mulatto* or the regrettable "high yaller." He had admired them because they were so different. Ozzie's hair was wildly curly to a fault, and her skin was more olive than coffee, but her nose was straight and her lips at least fuller than his.

To say he admired Ozzie Washington was to minimize the matter. He was no expert, but Colm thought he loved her. He had met her seven years ago in 1875, when the Fourth Infantry was first garrisoned at Fort Laramie. The Medical Department had assigned Colm permanent duty there—barring field emergencies—so he had ample time to watch the movements of various regiments. Ozzie stood out because the hospital had been plagued with endless winter ailments, and then-Major Chambers, commanding, ordered her there to help.

Help she had. Ozzie had no fear of the pukes or runs and did exactly what the surgeons required. She never complained, and she kept her mouth closed when other women on similar assignments objected long and loud.

During a welcome lull in sheet changing and basin dumping, Colm had mustered his courage and asked her how she remained so calm. She had given him a kind look, the sort of glance women reserved for the young and the addled, and said in her velvet voice, "Suh, if I didn't help, who would?"

She was right. Colm assured her that he was no sir, just a hospital steward. She nodded with understanding, but everlastingly called him "suh." He quit arguing about it, because he liked the languid way one word glided into the next when she spoke.

Ozzie Washington was exotic to Colm Callahan, who himself was an orphan from New York's bleak Five Points slum, a drummer boy with the Irish Brigade, who had become an impromptu hospital steward at Gettysburg, when he had no choice—much like Ozzie.

Her kindness stood out more than her beauty. He remembered an endless night in 1876 when the post surgeon had stretched out onto the table in his operating bay to grab a nap. Colm had slumped to the wall in the corridor, weary nigh unto death of 36-hour days. With a tap on his shoulder, Ozzie had handed him a cup of tea and an apple already sliced, then sat beside him. When he forgot to eat, she put a slice in his hand. So kind.

Once he had mentioned her to a friend, a corporal in the Third Cavalry, tentatively expressing himself. The corporal had looked at him in shock.

"You know what she is," the man had said, then said it anyway—a word Colm heard all the time, and had probably said a few times himself; everyone did. After that day, he never said it again, because it wasn't a polite way to talk about someone as thoughtful as Ozzie Washington.

Any fears the corporal would blab to others that the Irish hospital steward was enamored with a maid of color ended at the Battle of the Rosebud, where the corporal died. Colm had never chanced his feelings again; he kept his thoughts about Ozzie to himself. He was too shy to ever act on them.

Still, during moments like this at the window, he wondered what he would do when the Fourth Infantry was ordered somewhere else and Ozzie went along as Mrs. Lieutenant Colonel Chambers's trusted maid. When that happened, as it inevitably would, all he had left was resignation, leaving the army far behind. Another encounter with Ozzie would be more punishment than a shy man deserved.

Also before the story begins

Ozzie Washington knew it was time to visit the post office. Three weeks had passed since she had given her letter to a private in A Company, Fifth Cavalry, and asked him to mail it for her when the troop reached Fort Russell in Cheyenne. He'd never asked questions, because he couldn't read, and she always gave him a dime for her errand. He would mail the letter she had addressed to Audra Washington, Fort Laramie, Wyoming Territory, which would arrive back here in a week or so.

The first time she had mailed herself a letter, the Fourth had been garrisoned in Fort Concho, Texas. Lieutenant Colonel Chambers, then a captain, had checked the mail, staring a long time at the envelope.

"Audra Washington? Who do we know named Audra Washington?" he had joked.

"My real name is Audra," Ozzie had said.

He hadn't handed the letter to her until he teased her about a beau, which made her smile. She had no beau. Even when the Fourth had been garrisoned with one of the colored regiments, she never had one; she was too white for those men, even if they were former slaves too. The corporals and sergeants of the white regiments considered her too dark for them. There would never be a beau.

She never wrote herself more than four letters a year. When the day's work was done, she would make herself tea and open the letter she had written to herself. "Dearest Little Audra," she always began, as if this letter were from her mother, an illiterate woman who had been sold away from her, screaming, when Audra was only five, and sent to an East Texas cotton plantation. In these letters, this mother she barely remembered was living as a seamstress in New Orleans, with her own shop and an elegant clientele.

As the years passed, Ozzie wove an intricate fiction of carpetbaggers and a fine man who courted her widowed mother, leaving her his fortune when he died of yellow fever. Her letters to herself were fabulous, and a welcome treat, because she had no one and would never have received a letter otherwise.

Mrs. Lieutenant Colonel Chambers was always happy to have Ozzie make the trip to the post office. While it couldn't be said that Hattie Chambers was lazy, it could be said that she cared not to exert herself, especially in high summer when the wind blew, as it invariably did in Wyoming Territory. Ozzie knew the trick of weighting the hem of her dresses with fishing lures or lead shot, the better to fool the wind.

Seventeen years in the employ of the same family meant that Ozzie had them all well trained. The Chambers' children had been trundled off to relatives in the East for schooling, which meant that life in the lieutenant colonel's quarters was simple. When her chores were done, she was at her leisure to walk to the post office.

She tried to time her visit with the probable appearance of Hospital Steward Colm Callahan, but lately he had been less cooperative. Either the post surgeon was picking up his own mail, or the dratted man had given Suh other duties.

She always thought of Steward Callahan as Suh. Face red, he had told her once that he was no gentleman, so she needn't refer to him that way. She had been just brave enough to continue calling him Suh, until he no longer objected. After that non-introduction, they had settled into the familiarity of frontier service, nothing more.

Ozzie admired the way he looked, even if his nose did peel in the summer, and he was too vain (or busy) to coat it with zinc oxide, as some of the other light-skinned men did. He burned and peeled regularly, which detracted in no way from his admirable height and high cheekbones, which gave his face a thin look. His eyes were a surprising brown rather than the expected blue. In a moment of rare candor for a man so reticent, Suh had remarked that her eyes were lighter than his. The fact that he'd noticed flattered her.

He once told her how much he enjoyed the gentle flow of her Louisiana accent, but she never worked up the nerve to tell him that she liked the clipped cadence of his New York speak with just a hint of the Irish. That his grammar was impeccable, even though he admitted his early years were spent in a ghastly orphanage, hinted something else: he was as ambitious as she was.

Her own ambition had been borne of desperation. Maybe someday she would tell Suh about those dark days as the war was ending. Thinking back, she knew that the time a war was winding down was the worst time of all.

While it was true that the port of New Orleans had been liberated by Yankees early in the game, coloreds on the state's northern plantations had lingered in slavery. Ozzie thought she was twelve when the other slaves had simply dropped their tools or untied their aprons and walked off the LeCheminant plantation with not a word spoken. She remembered feeble protests from Madame LeCheminant and her daughters. What could they do, with all of the white men gone fighting in Lee's army?

Ozzie was young, so she'd stayed and found herself saddled with all of the house chores the others had done. When it became too much, she knotted her other dress in a tablecloth, along with her rosary and an ebony-backed hairbrush she'd swiped from Lalage LeCheminant, a child her own age, whose companion she had been. Lalage had been the first to call her Ozzie because she could not pronounce Audra.

At twelve, Ozzie had slung her tablecloth luggage over her shoulder and left the house just after dark, when the haunts were out, which she did not believe in, being of a practical mind. A kindly man of color with a load of chickens trussed for market handed her up beside him in his cart and shared his sandwich with her.

He told her to find a Yankee woman to work for, that the best place was the US Army encampment where he was headed. When they arrived outside New Orleans two days later in the early-evening rain, he helped her down and pointed to a row of houses, Officers Row.

She knocked on the first door, tried to introduce herself, and received a swipe with a broom for her pains. At the second door, she introduced herself, recited her skills—some exaggerated, some not—and did not leave even when Mrs. Captain Chambers closed the door politely on her. She shivered on the porch through the night and was still there in the morning when Captain Chambers looked out the window and saw her, chin up and eyes determined, a child.

He let her in, and she'd been their servant ever since. Ozzie Washington worked hard at every task assigned her and saved her modest wages, which were paid every other month when the army was paid. She never looked back.

Maybe it was time to put that money to use. She'd liked the look of Cheyenne—it was more refined since the early days, when the rowdy Union Pacific crew went through. The days were gone when she could knock on a door, look both desperate and determined, and find work. She had true skill now in dressmaking.

Any day, she would bid the Chambers *au revoir*, catch the southbound stage at the Rustic Hotel, and land herself in Cheyenne. Every town of any size had a seamstress or two. She could find work with one of the dressmakers, see where the land lay, and start her own business.

Any day.

Where the story actually begins

"Things are slow, Callahan. If I have to treat one more case of diarrhea, I'll take to drink," Captain Dilworth had announced one morning.

Colm was far too wise to say that he alone had treated those so afflicted, because it was a homely duty beneath the notice of the post surgeon. As for taking to drink, Captain Dilworth was already lurching down that road. Again, Colm was too wise to mention it.

"Captain, are you thinking about a bolt to Cheyenne?" he asked instead.

"I was thinking more in terms of Omaha with the missus. We'll catch the UP in Cheyenne and spend a week there. Can you manage? I expect no trouble."

Yet again, Colm was far too experienced to suggest that the nature of medicine often meant a nasty surprise now and then, something beyond the official duties of a hospital steward. But who was he kidding? In the absence of post surgeons, Colm had extracted arrows, set bones, pulled teeth, prescribed probably useless medicine, done a successful shoulder resection because someone had to, and had even delivered a stubborn baby.

"I can manage, sir. When are you leaving?"

They had been through this conversation several times since Captain Dilworth had arrived three years ago. Colm had worked with better surgeons before, and worse ones. He could handle a hospital in a backwater garrison for a week.

The Dilworths were gone in a day, which made Colm Callahan happy; he liked being in charge. He had stood by his favorite window, looking down on the venerable fort below. "Bring it on, Old Girl," he boasted.

A day later, Colm Callahan wished he hadn't tempted Asclepius, the Greek god of medicine. That day began long before days should, with banging on his door by a frightened first-time father, a lieutenant of cavalry with the Fifth. Colm was pulling up his suspenders before the man finished knocking.

"My wife isn't due for confinement for another six weeks, but . . . but, there's water everywhere!"

So there was. When Colm arrived, Mrs. Lieutenant looked as frightened as her husband; he had two youngsters to calm down. He sent the lieutenant running down Officers Row to the Chambers' quarters with a note for Ozzie. Five minutes later, she arrived, and the calming began. Ten minutes later, the sheets and Mrs. Lieutenant were changed and the mother-to-be was back in bed. In another twenty, there was an addition to the dependents at Fort Laramie, a little one who looked almost as surprised as her parents.

"Nothing's ready!" the mother wailed.

"Heavens," Ozzie said so calmly. "All we need is a bureau drawer and some toweling." She turned to Colm. "Or should we put this little one close to the kitchen range, Suh?"

"My thought precisely," Colm said, happy he had been so wise to summon Ozzie.

While Ozzie laid a fire in the wood stove and pulled up a chair padded with a quilt, Colm cleaned the infant. "We'll keep her warm by the fire for a few days," he explained. "She's a wee one and could use a boost. Happily, 'tis summer. And what will you name her?"

Soon Eugenia Victoria—so much of a name for one so small—had gathered herself into a compact bundle and slept, warm, before the open oven door. When all was calm at the lieutenant's, and Sergeant Flaherty's wife was in firm control there, Colm thanked Ozzie. With a nod, she started back to the Chambers' quarters. He stood a moment looking at her, a smile on his face.

That night, he managed forty-five minutes of sleep before the bugler sounded sick call. Luckily there was only a bilious stomach and a hacking cough to deal with before the next emergency, an ankle avulsion caused when a soldier-turned-carpenter (the army hated to pay for experts when privates existed) fell off a partly shingled stable roof.

His comrades carried the private to the hospital on a stretcher as he moaned and clutched the offending ankle. The private timed his arrival with the appearance of a baker's assistant who had spilled hot grease on his forearm. Colm sighed and wrote another note, sent with one of the stretcher men. By the time Ozzie arrived, the owner of the avulsed ankle was certain that amputation lay in his immediate future, and the baker's assistant had fainted when Colm touched his arm.

Sensible Ozzie. "Where do you need me the most, Suh?" The sparkle in her eyes betrayed her amusement, but she looked serious enough to satisfy the patients.

Without thinking, Colm put his hand on her shoulder. "The ankle thinks he's facing amputation at his hip and sure death. Calm him down while I take care of the burn."

She went to her duty while Colm made no attempt to revive the burn. Better to clean and prod while the man was in a far better place.

Burns in the second degree, he thought as he went to work. Out of the corner of his eye, Colm watched Ozzie remove the avulsed ankle's shoes. She wiped the man's face with a damp cloth, all the while keeping up a soothing conversation. Soon he was silent, caught in Ozzie's web. What a gift.

When the burn was resting with a cold compress on his arm, Colm pulled up a stool and sat by Ozzie's patient, whose eyes filled with terror again.

"By the Merciful, steward! Don't take off my leg!"

"Wouldn't dream of it," Colm said. "But I'm going to poke a bit. The pretty lady will hold your hand."

The pretty lady did so, freeing Colm to let his experienced fingers roam around a rapidly swelling ankle. "Wiggle your toes," he commanded, and the private wiggled. *This little piggy*, Colm thought. "Once more."

The private looked at him expectantly, but when Colm just sat there, the dread returned.

"Not a break in sight, private," he announced, putting the man out of some of his misery. "There's an avulsion, though, which means a little piece of bone has been tugged away by the ligament. We'll treat it with RICE."

The soldier stared at him. "Rice?"

"Aye, lad." Colm ticked off four fingers on his hand. "R-I-C-E: rest, ice, compression, and elevation. And no more roofs, d'ye hear? I'll send a note to the sergeant."

"Yes, sir!" The private closed his eyes with relief, certain he had stared down death.

After the man was resting, iced, compressed, and elevated, Colm promenaded from the ward to the entrance with the woman who had come to his aid twice today. He walked as slowly as he could, although he knew Ozzie had other duties. He was too shy to ask her to return later if she could, but he needn't have bothered.

"I'll be back this evening to sit with your patients," she said. She peered closer; clearly more was on her mind.

"Go ahead," he said, wishing she would reveal her undying love.

No luck. "Suh, do you think you should telegraph Fort Russell for some help? At the very least, where's your hospital matron?"

"Home with lumbago," he said and made a face. "As for telegraphing, I don't think conditions here will get much worse."

Things did get much worse a half hour later, after Mess Call. As the hospital matron had hauled her bones up the hill to prepare lunch, the bugler sounded sick call, something that never happened at one o'clock in the afternoon.

Captain Dilworth had left his medical bag in his office. Colm grabbed it and was out the door in seconds. He ran down the hill toward a crowd gathered by the post traders' complex.

From its off-colored front wheels, he recognized the ambulance as the vehicle that had left for Cheyenne only that morning, carrying mail and several officers bound for court-martial duty. Colm worked his way through the crowd to the sergeant on patrol, a usually genial Irishman like himself who looked anything but genial.

"Colm, dear boyo, we came across the Shy-Dead stagecoach just past the iron bridge, tipped on its side." He gestured to a piece of canvas from which booted feet poked out. "Couldn't do anything for the driver." He pointed again, further inside the ambulance. "Here's your real patient."

Ever cautious, Colm raised the canvas. The driver's neck was cocked at an odd angle, but Colm rested his fingers against it anyway. Nothing. He shook his head.

"Come, come, young man, I am yet alive!"

Colm stared in surprise at the huge voice that boomed from an older man of somewhat ordinary dimensions. He wore a suit that could be called flashy—odd in a man of obvious mature years. Colm looked closer. The man's cravat was a strident shade of green that would give a statue a headache. Stuck through it was a cravat pin in the shape of tragedy and comedy masks.

"Lysander Locke, the Lysander Locke, awaiting your good offices, sir!" the man boomed again. "I do believe I have broken my leg."

"I . . . well . . . let me look." Colm moved farther into the ambulance.

Colm felt the leg. The man was entirely correct. Lysander Locke's tibia appeared to be at odds with the world. To his relief, the skin was still intact.

Lysander Locke watched Colm's gentle prodding with a real air of detachment, even as he sucked in his breath. "Say it isn't serious and that I can be on my way to Deadwood, where an engagement awaits to perform *King Lear* in three days."

Colm smiled; he couldn't help himself. The man spoke in such theatrical tones, with a certain flourish. He was worlds braver than the avulsed ankle resting in the hospital.

"It is most certainly a broken leg, so Shakespeare will have to wait a few weeks."

Lysander Locke put the back of his hand to his forehead, and closed his eyes. "Young man, the show must go on!"

"Not in the next three days."

His hand still on the broken leg, Colm took a good look at his patient, doubting that Fort Laramie had ever seen such a man. "Otherwise, how are you?"

"A little shaken, my good man, but none the worse for it," the man announced. "I am Lysander Locke, late of Drury Lane and Covent Gardens, and a noted tragedian."

Not one to hide your light under a bushel, Colm thought, amused.

Lysander Locke had an accent, but Colm didn't think he would have placed it so close to England. But never mind. Here was a man with a broken leg, even though Captain Dilworth had

42

assured him that nothing would happen while he was in Omaha.

The medical department does not pay me enough, Colm thought as he scribbled another note to Ozzie.

"Let's get up the hill," he told the driver as he crouched next to his newest patient.

With a passing private's help, Colm loaded the corpse onto a stretcher and left him in the solitude of the dead house, located behind the hospital and next to his own little quarters. The same stretcher moved Lysander Locke into the hospital's operating bay, if Colm could call such a place where no one had operated in recent memory.

Thank goodness Ozzie arrived so promptly. Without a word, Colm handed her one of his own aprons, which circled her waist and then some.

"Are you game, Ozzie?" he asked when she stood outside the operating bay, looking indecisive. "We'll need to cut away his trousers and smallclothes. I don't want to shock you or anything . . ."

Maybe this was a stupid idea. Holding patients' hands was one thing, but asking her to assist an operation quite another. "Or maybe I should do this myself."

"I'm no shrinking violet, Suh," was all she said as she crooked her arm through his and towed him into the operating bay.

Indeed she was not. Ozzie did everything he asked, all the while delicately covering the actor with a sheet. Praise all the Saints and the Almighty that the fracture was a simple one. Just the right amount of chloroform on a square of gauze put him out so Colm could go to work, rotating and straightening, comparing the two legs, tinkering until he was satisfied.

"You're as good as Captain Dilworth," Ozzie said, holding the leg still while he splinted it. "Probably better. You've done a lot of this, haven't you?"

Maybe he was feeling cocky because the whole matter went so smoothly. Whatever the reason, he told Ozzie about the night on the battlefield five years ago at White Mountain. He had assisted Captain Sternberg, who operated by feel in the dark, because Nez Perce sharpshooters kept targeting their kerosene lamp. "We both worked on that man and saved him, all in the dark," he concluded, as he finished splinting. Plaster would come later.

"You're a hero, Suh."

"Just a hospital steward. Pull him toward you a bit."

When he finished, they rolled the table into the wardroom. The avulsed ankle and burned forearm watched with some interest as the two of them gently lowered the actor into a bed.

"I'll sit with him until he comes around," Colm said. "The matron promised to return with food for him, but I have my doubts." He looked at the lovely woman beside him, who was watching the actor. "Ozzie, I do need you."

"Then you have me, Suh," she said quietly. "Mrs. Chambers will manage."

"It'll be more than a night or two," he said, doubtful again.

"She'll manage," she replied so softly, touched his shoulder, and left the ward.

He watched her walk away, embarrassed that he had boasted about that battlefield surgery. It was all true, but he had never been a man to toot his horn. He couldn't help wondering when she would get tired of helping him.

"That is a lovely woman."

Colm looked around in surprise. The stentorian voice, which could probably blow out the back wall of a theatre, was considerably weakened, but there was no mistaking the dramatic timbre.

"You're among the living again," he said, putting a hand against the old gent's chest. "Firm beat." He touched his two fingers to his wrist. "True there."

To his further surprise, the actor grabbed Colm's wrist and inexpertly felt for a pulse. "Lad, are you smitten by that pretty lady?" He closed his eyes. "When I feel better, you must tell me everything."

When pigs fly, Colm thought, not sure if he was amused or exasperated. *Gadfreys, was he that obvious to a man coming out of anesthesia?*

As it turned out, Ozzie didn't have to exert any pressure on her employer. She explained the situation, and Mrs. Chambers barely heard anything beyond *actor*.

"Do you think he might perform for us when he is better?" she asked. "We could hold such a party."

"It'll be a few days until he is lively enough," Ozzie hedged. "Surely you can arrange for a corporal's wife to help out while I am busy at the hospital." She delivered the clincher. "It's for the good of the regiment."

Mrs. Chambers was no slouch, and no kinder than most penny-pinchers. "If you will promise her the wages I would have paid you."

"Yes, indeed," Ozzie replied, secretly amused.

As she hurried to her little room to gather up an apron that fit, and her extra dress, Ozzie stopped a moment to pat her hair here and there, then wonder how long she might have to stay at the hospital. It would be a pleasant change from garrison tedium, if nothing else. She patted her hair a little more.

All was calm in the hospital when Ozzie returned. She hesitated in the corridor, wondering if Suh really needed her.

She sniffed the air. He needed her. She peeked into the kitchen. There he stood, stirring madly at a pot from which a burned smell rose like gas in a Louisiana swamp.

"I'm hopeless," he said. "The books say patients should have a low diet of gruel and tea, but for the life of me . . ."

He took the pan off the hob, looked inside hopefully, as if something might have changed, and sighed.

Without a word, he handed her the wooden spoon, turned around and bent over, which made Ozzie whoop with laughter. Soon, he laughed too.

"Help me?" he asked simply, straightening up. "I have eggs, milk, and cream." He looked toward the pot. "We'll forget the farina."

Ozzie carried the offending pan to the dry sink and left it there to suffer third-degree burns. "We may have to throw out that pan altogether," she said. "I will cook for you all."

Suh put his hand to his heart and staggered backward. "Thank the Almighty." Perhaps he had learned something from Lysander Locke, Shakespeare tragedian. "'We,' she says. 'We.' She's not leaving me alone to suffer."

Ozzie wiped tears of merriment from her eyes. "I am going to make scrambled eggs and flapjacks."

"That's not a low diet."

"Honestly, Suh, how can anyone get well on gruel?"

"So I've tried to tell any number of post surgeons in the past decade, with no success." He looked around elaborately. "But Captain Dilworth isn't here, and those men are hungry."

"Then stand back and let me cook," she said. "Any vanilla? Dare I ask for maple syrup?"

"You dare, indeed." He pointed out the objects in question. "I will retreat to the ward and assure the broken leg, burned arm, and avulsed ankle that good food will arrive shortly, and that I had nothing to do with it."

Smiling, she went to work in the hospital kitchen, grateful for the matron's lumbago. The kitchen was well stocked and quiet. Ozzie found herself humming as she made flapjacks, that staple of army life, but with a touch of vanilla. They went into the warming oven while she scrambled eggs and added cream, something even the Chambers didn't see in their kitchen too often. Medical rations were far superior, as long as amateur cooks weren't allowed to roam at will, like Suh.

"Suh, you are a forlorn hope in the kitchen," she said to the eggs, which were getting all glossy, as good scrambled eggs should.

She found a small cart on wheels, so it was with her own Louisiana flair that she rolled dinner into the ward and witnessed the eagerness of hungry men.

Poor, poor Mr. Lysander Locke. His eyes were half open in the same sickroom stare she recalled from times of illness in the Chambers household. She was hard pressed to remember a time she had ever been bedridden. Sick, yes, but that meant nothing on a plantation, unless you were white. She looked at the peaceful men lying there, wondering why others were born to serve.

"Pancakes and scrambled eggs, gentlemen," she said, certain that three of the four had never been called *gentlemen* before.

The hospital steward's relief was nearly palpable, to Ozzie's delight. As Colm helped the avulsed ankle into a sitting position, the burn looked on with interest. "I can't remember when I last saw maple syrup," he declared, pushing himself upright.

Soon the soldiers were eating. Ozzie voiced no objection when the burn asked permission to douse even his eggs in maple syrup.

Lysander Locke was more of a challenge. As Colm struggled to help him sit up, Locke sighed in a most theatrical way.

"You'd better lend a hand too, my dear miss," the actor said.

She obliged, quietly pleased when Colm twined his fingers with hers and offered a firmer foundation to a man more substantial than the usual run-of-the-mill soldier. They hauled Lysander Locke upright. If the steward kept his fingers twined in hers a little longer than a casual observer may have thought necessary, Ozzie still had no objection. Their heads were close together too. Colm Callahan smelled strangely of camphor, which puzzled her. Camphor?

She gently released her grip on Colm and stepped back, but Lysander Locke plucked her sleeve. "Do I ask too much, my dear, to ask you to feed me? I feel so weak."

Ozzie looked at the steward, who nodded. His eyes were full of concern, and made her wonder if she had become entirely too cynical at the advanced age of twenty-eight.

Mr. Locke is not at death's door, she thought.

"I dislike eating alone," her patient said as she tucked a napkin under his chin. "Is there enough for this fine young man too?" he asked, indicating Colm.

"Yes, Suh," she said. "We'll need another plate."

That fine young man took the cue and hurried to the kitchen, returning with two plates and forks. "There's enough for all of us," he said, taking his share and dishing a plate for her. "We can take turns feeding him."

They did. Before long, the actor was regaling them with stories of fame and fortune in Drury Lane, and then Broadway. But it wasn't entirely about him. After the scrambled eggs were gone, he paused in his narrative.

"Laddie, you have a faint accent that places you in New York City, and perhaps somewhere more removed."

"Aye," Colm said. Ozzie smiled as he blushed. Such a shy man. "The farther removed is County Kerry, which I left at the tender age of five."

"Thence to the teeming metropolis of lower Manhattan?"

Colm nodded, his expression more serious. "You needn't know any more."

"But I wish to," Lysander Locke said. He indicated Ozzie. "And so does this fair damsel, who saved us from starvation. By the way, my dear, what is your place of origin?"

"A plantation in Louisiana," she told him. "It belonged to the LeCheminant family, but it might be in the hands of a bank now, or maybe a Yankee scalawag."

"I see no regret," Colm commented, his eyes lively.

"None from me, Suh." She could have told him much more, but she didn't need his sympathy, and she didn't know the actor well enough to need his, either. As a house slave, she had been treated kindly enough, discounting the times Madam LeCheminant took after her with a hairbrush when Ozzie had talked back to Madam LeCheminant's daughter. She still had scars on her back and neck.

Lysander Locke looked at them. "Here I am, stove up and wounded and relying on you both to entertain me, but you're struck dumb!"

Ozzie glanced at Colm and started to laugh, just a quiet one, because she had been taught years ago to call no attention to herself. But she couldn't help herself when Colm turned away, his shoulders shaking. She laughed louder, until she was leaning against the iron footboard of the actor's bed.

"*What* is so funny?" Lysander demanded finally, with all the careful enunciation and drama he probably saved for the stage.

Colm recovered first. "It's this way, sir. Speaking for myself, I've never considered myself an entertainer." He turned his smile on Ozzie. "Miss Washington? Have you ever been asked to entertain someone?"

"I have, Suh," she said, her voice soft. As she braved a glance at Colm Callahan, she saw a flicker of understanding in his eyes. Where it came from and how, she did not know, but it gave her courage to continue. "I was the personal slave and entertainer of Lalage LeCheminant, who was five years old, my age. If I couldn't entertain her, I got the hairbrush for my pains."

Colm's smile vanished. She'd said too much and turned to go, but he touched her elbow. That was it, nothing more. She had long suspected that Colm Callahan may have had a less-than-pleasant childhood of his own. Too bad she would never be brave enough to ask about it.

She recovered as gracefully as she could, looking down at the little watch pinned to her bodice. "Dear me, Suh, I think your other patients need more flapjacks." With all the poise she could muster, she pushed the cart down the row toward the other men.

Colm seated himself so he could at least pretend to listen to Lysander Locke, and still keep an eye on Ozzie Washington. He already knew that the actor could carry on a conversation requiring little from the listener save the occasional *aye* and nod.

Locke was saying something about the importance of being in Deadwood within a day or two as Colm watched Ozzie finish serving flapjacks and retreat to the kitchen.

"I will have you know that I once served in the Swiss Guard and saved Pope Pius from assassination by cutting a man's throat with my teeth."

"Aye, sir," Colm said, which earned him a balled up napkin thrown at his temple, followed by a theatrical laugh aimed at the back wall.

"Ah ha! I could have told you I was Judas himself, and you'd have nodded," Lysander Locke declared with triumph. "You're not paying attention. You're a goner, did you know?"

"I . . . what?" Colm asked, embarrassed.

Locke's voice turned into a stage whisper. "Laddie, I know a smitten man when I see one."

Colm sighed, deciding then and there not to reenlist in September. When even a moth-eaten old actor could see right through him, it was time to take up another line of work in a distant city, perhaps Constantinople. Colm waited a moment, knowing that his good humor would return. It did, but not as soon as usual.

"You're right, sir," he said, knowing it would be foolish to argue with a patient who would be gone in a week or less. "I've admired Ozzie Washington for years, but—"

"You've made no move because she is a woman of color?" the actor supplied.

Colm started in surprise. "Not at all!" he exclaimed, wanting to brain the man with a bedpan for such an observation. He was tired;

that was it. How had he gotten himself into this discussion?

"Then why are you wasting time?"

Colm opened his mouth to make some stupid reply, then closed it. "I have things to do," he mumbled, and left the ward. In the hall, he leaned against the wall and closed his eyes. What had happened? He was precise and efficient for 364 days a year, until the 365th, when an actor showed up with a broken leg.

"Are you all right, Suh?" Ozzie had such a lovely voice, and she even sounded concerned.

He could have made some noncommittal reply—yesterday, he probably would have—but something had changed. He just wasn't certain what. The earth's axis hadn't shifted, and as far as he knew, no out-of-control meteor raced toward Wyoming Territory. He could go upstairs and busy himself with something, except that he didn't want to. He wanted to stay in the corridor with Ozzie.

"Suh?"

"Never been better," he told her, and it might have been true. Deep breath. "You know I need help. Ozzie, I'm about to fall asleep." He shifted to look her in the eye. "Am I asking too much of you?"

Bless her heart, she knew just what he meant. Trust a woman to know. "We're going to take turns here," she said, and he heard some uncertainty. "I sort of wish you would be closer than your quarters, in case something happens, but I know you need to sleep."

"Let's do this: While you're in the ward, I'll sleep on the cot in Captain Dilworth's office." No point in standing on overmuch ceremony. "I . . . I changed my bed linens yesterday, so you can sleep in my house while I'm awake in here."

She nodded, practical as he was. She turned to say something when a moan came from the ward. Ozzie's eyes opened wide in fright, but then she giggled. "He's such an . . . an actor," she whispered, leaning toward Colm. "I'll see what's wrong."

He nodded, content to let her do his dirty work, because he was a most typical man. She returned a moment later. "I have been requested to keep Mistuh Locke company," she said. "You, Suh, get to wash the dishes."

"And I shall," he said. "Then I will go to bed. I'll take the cot in Captain Dilworth's office while you watch in the ward."

A worried frown appeared between her eyes. Impulsively, he smoothed it down with gentle fingers. "If anything happens, just knock on Captain Dilworth's door. I won't be far." She gave him a relieved smile, which warmed his heart.

Before sitting beside the actor, Ozzie did her own ward walk, something she had seen Suh do. The private with the avulsed ankle was full of flapjacks and settling himself down for the night. When she rested the back of her hand against his forehead, he opened his eyes.

She glanced at the chart hanging at the foot of his bed. "Is everything all right, Private Henry?" she asked. "If you need something, just call me."

He nodded and closed his eyes. Private Jones with the burned forearm was in some pain. "I'll ask Steward Callahan if there is something—"

A mighty crash of pans came from the kitchen.

"You may want to trade places with the steward for a few minutes," Private Jones suggested. "He doesn't shine around crockery."

She laughed and took his suggestion. With some relief, Suh turned over the dishes to her. "Let me measure powders any day," he muttered as he hurried from the kitchen.

He returned sometime later as she made her last swipe of the dish towel around the last plate. "My timing is exquisite," he joked. "I've administered powders and done bedpan duty," he said, ticking the items off on his fingers. "Two out of three are asleep, and you must listen to the actor for a while. G'night."

He tipped an imaginary hat to her. A moment later, she heard the door to Captain Dilworth's office close.

He had left a kerosene lamp on the table in the corridor, a hospital lamp with four slatted sides for varying degrees of light. On the back of a blank prescription, she found a note. *Take this with you,* Suh had scrawled.

Ozzie closed two of the slats and carried the lamp into the ward. Feeling like Florence

Nightingale at Scutari Hospital, she held it high and satisfied herself that the privates slumbered. Lysander Locke was wide awake. She pulled up a chair, made herself comfortable, and asked him why he couldn't sleep.

"I am an actor. We are always awake in the evening. Curtain comes down at ten of the clock."

"And then you sleep?"

"No, no. I smile graciously at well-wishers, remove my makeup, then toddle off to a nearby chophouse. In New York City, I take a hansom cab to Delmonico's."

She couldn't overlook the wistful tone in his voice. "It's been a while since New York City?" she asked, then could have bitten her tongue, because it sounded so heartless.

Lysander Locke sighed. Maybe he was more tired than he wanted to let on. "Far too long, my dear," he said. "Denver wasn't quite the cultural center I was led to believe."

He didn't say it with any self-pity, but Ozzie knew what he meant. She could have made some offhand remark, but something had happened between them. She wasn't certain just what, but maybe it was her turn to talk. She took a deep breath.

"I know how that feels. Freedom is nice, but it's not all that easy."

Her words, softly spoken, seemed to hang there like mist. She gathered her nerve and looked at Mr. Locke, wondering what he was thinking.

He gazed back, his eyes so kind, even though she knew he must be in pain. "How did freedom come to you, Miss Washington?"

She told him about borrowing courage from some unused source to finally walk away from the LeCheminant plantation. "I think I was twelve. My mother would know for sure, but she was sold into East Texas when I was five."

You can't possibly want to hear this, she thought, and started to rise. There must be something she could fold, or put away, or straighten, and this man did need his sleep. He put out his hand, motioning down, so she remained where she was.

"Sold? Your mother?"

Ozzie nodded, startled that her eyes should start to brim. She knew she would never find her mother, though she thought about her every day. "She was a house Negro. Maybe she made Madam LeCheminant angry."

"Your father?"

Ozzie shrugged. "Monsieur LeCheminant. That would explain the anger."

Mr. Locke made a sudden noise that didn't sound in the least theatrical.

"Never mind, Suh! That was life in the South."

Through the years, she had given the matter some thought. Maybe Mr. Locke would find it interesting.

"I don't know for certain, but I do know this: Whenever a new baby with light skin was born in the slave quarters, some house slave ended up on the auction block in Shreveport. Madame LeCheminant was not a kind woman. I have scars." She stopped, certain she had said too much. "Well, Suh, everyone has scars. Some show and some don't."

When Lysander Locke spoke, his voice shook. "Did you . . . did you choose your last name?"

"I did," she declared with pride, then looked around, fearful she had spoken too loud. Private

Henry shifted positions, but Private Jones continued to snore.

"I gather your choice wasn't LeCheminant?" the actor teased, but gently.

"Never," she said emphatically, but quieter. "Some chose Jackson, or Lincoln, or Jefferson. Others gave me all sorts of suggestions, but *I* wanted to choose something for the first time in my life. Washington freed his slaves. I like it."

"So do I, Miss Washington, but why Ozzie?"

"It's really Audra," she said with a laugh. "My mother named me, but Lalage LeCheminant called me Ozzie." How much of the truth did the actor need? "I insisted that my name was Audra and got the hairbrush for being impertinent. I'm used to Ozzie now."

"Do you never use Audra?" he asked. "It's lovely."

"Well . . ." She hadn't planned to tell him, but it was late, and she was tired. Maybe talking would keep her awake.

The two slats of the ward lamp gave off such a comforting glow. She could almost imagine herself sitting in front of a fire in her own parlor, if she had one.

"I pretend to get letters from my mother." For just a moment, the sorrow of the whole thing grabbed her. She had not seen her mother in twenty-three years; why should it matter now? She would have stopped if she hadn't seen such interest in the old actor's eyes. "I . . . I address it to Audra Washington and send it to myself."

"Right here?"

"I give it to a soldier heading to Cheyenne, or maybe Omaha, and he mails it from there. Or he may be going to Billings, in Montana Territory." She touched his hand. "Or even Deadwood! That way, I'm never quite certain when it will come back. Sometimes . . ." She paused again, hoping he would not think her foolish. "Sometimes I even forget, and the letter is almost a surprise. As if . . ."

"Your mother actually sent it," Lysander Locke finished. "You're a remarkable lady, Miss Washington." His voice was lower now, the words strung out. His eyes closed.

"Do you receive other letters, my dear?" he asked, when she thought he slept.

"Who would write to me?" This was becoming too serious; she had to turn the conversation.

"Mr. Locke, how does your mail keep up with you?"

He yawned. "My mail? I don't get much mail either."

It had never occurred to Ozzie that there were others like her.

"You hear from your family, don't you?"

"What family?"

"Well, I mean . . ."

He opened one eye. "I devoted myself to Shakespeare."

She couldn't think of anything to say to his artless declaration, mainly because she could not fathom anyone choosing such a life on purpose. How odd; how sad.

"Maybe someday you will settle down and have a family," she ventured cautiously.

No answer. She peered closer, hoping he would forget this entire conversation. Ozzie sat in silence as his breathing became regular and deep. *Poor man*, she thought as she stood.

Suh had draped Mr. Locke's clothes over the foot of the iron bedstead. Moving quietly, she took his suit coat and shook out the wrinkles, or tried to. The material wouldn't cooperate. She looked closer. The wool was cheap, even though it looked good from a distance. His bright green cravat had been creased and folded many times. How many cravats did Mr. Locke possess, or was this his only one? She put the coat on a peg reserved for patients' clothing and wet her fingers to smooth out the cravat.

He had a shabby little suitcase; perhaps he had other trousers. She gave the suit her critical appraisal: shiny wool with what looked like bits of filler fabric woven in.

"Mistuh Locke," she whispered, "fortune has not smiled on you lately."

Ozzie had seen better shirts in those rummage sales so dear to the hearts of army personnel. Since officers had to pay their own freight from garrison to garrison, any move of significance meant rummage sales to help lighten the load. She had acquired her second-best petticoat that way, as well as the shoes she wore now.

After a good wash, she could turn the cuffs on Mr. Locke's shirt. His stockings were hopeless, with holes in each heel, but she had yarn and could knit him another pair, considering that she'd be spending nights sitting in the ward so Suh could sleep a little.

She contemplated the matter as she walked up and down the little ward, stopping for a while beside the private with the burned arm. He moved restlessly, even though he was unconscious; his arm surely pained him. She hesitated at first then took his good hand in hers, stroking it until he settled into deeper sleep again.

She returned to her chair beside the actor, wondering how on earth he would fare in Deadwood, Dakota Territory. She had heard some of the garrisons' wives whisper about what a sinful place it was, with gambling, dance hall girls, and women of the night. She could not picture *King Lear* in such a place.

Are you telling us the truth, the whole truth, and nothing but the truth? she thought, then sighed. Who would lie about Deadwood?

She must have dozed, because she woke up to a light hand on her shoulder. Was it already two o'clock? Startled, she looked up to see Suh holding a finger to his lips, his eyes lively even in the gloom. He looked more chipper than a man should with so little sleep, but Ozzie knew he was used to the twilight life of a hospital steward.

"Everyone alive?" he asked, bending close to her ear.

"Suh, you see them in the same state you left them," she retorted, enjoying his little joke—and the way his breath warmed her ear and set off prickles down her spine.

He pointed to the door, and she followed. The door to Captain Dilworth's office stood open, and moonlight streamed into the corridor. A portrait of poor President Garfield still hung there. Any day now, someone from Washington, DC, would surely remember to mail a portrait of President Arthur.

Tired now, she stood next to President Garfield, glad to turn the patients over to someone who could do them more good than she if they woke.

"How long should I sleep?" she asked.

"Until Mess Call." He made a face. "Wish it could be longer, but you know my kitchen skills."

She just smiled.

"I'll tend to sick call, and then make sure our patients are buffed and sparkling before I turn them over to you again," he joked.

"And?" she prompted, when he seemed to hesitate.

"Ordinarily, I'd let you take another rest before Noon Mess, but I have to attend to the corpse in the dead house."

"Glory, Suh, do you *embalm* too?"

"I am a man of amazing talents, Ozzie. Learned that skill in the war, as well as others."

Suh took her arm and guided her to the side door, opening it onto a moonlit path. "Enough of that indelicate subject! I'll wait right here until you go inside." He indicated the two little buildings, pointing to the left. "That's mine. The other one's the dead house." He chuckled. "Don't mix them up."

She stopped halfway down the path and took a few steps back toward him. He met her, a question in his eyes.

"Suh, I wonder just how successful Mr. Locke really is. His suit looks like it's made of shoddy, and why on earth would anyone in Deadwood want to see *King Lear*?"

"I've been wondering that myself," he replied. "D'ye think he's putting on an act for us?"

She shrugged.

"If he wakes up with the chickens, I'll see what I can learn. Go to bed, Ozzie. You've been more than kind."

True to his word, he watched her until she stood on the porch of his quarters. His solicitude touched her. It wasn't more than a stone's throw to his quarters, but there he stood until she turned the doorknob.

"Lock the door," he called. "This is still an army garrison."

He had left a lamp burning in the small parlor. Even though she was ready to drop from exhaustion, Ozzie took the lamp and peered into his even smaller kitchen, which was tidy to the point of appearing unused. Considering his culinary skills—something he obviously hadn't learned in the war—she figured he ate his meals in the hospital, when the matron wasn't suffering from lumbago.

The other room was his bedchamber, with its narrow bed, three-drawer bureau, and a washbasin with a scrap of mirror at Suh-height for shaving. His night table had a lamp and two books: *Les Miserables* and the US Medical Department Annual Report, more well-thumbed than Jean Valjean's tale of woe and redemption.

No pictures hung on the walls in either room. The only thing she had noticed was a calendar of fetching, round-bottomed women in the kitchen. Suh had no more family than she did, a realization that saddened her.

Her eyes closed, Ozzie stripped down to her shimmy and crawled into bed. It was lumpy in all the right places, but the pillow smelled of that mysterious camphor. Her last thought was that she would have to ask him why on earth camphor.

Everyone slept, giving Colm time for the paperwork so dear to his heart. He discovered it was less dear than usual, mainly because he was picturing Ozzie Washington asleep in his bed. He was an organized, rational, intelligent, and efficient man. Even during those fraught days at the age of fourteen, when he stood beside his commanding officer in K Company, 69th Regiment of the Irish Brigade, drumming out the commands to direct soldiers into battle, he had not flinched or failed anyone. And here he was at thirty-four, a non-commissioned officer commanding some respect—mooning over a woman.

Dashed good thing I told you to lock the door, he thought in disgust. *I am an idiot.*

He was also disgusted with himself, too shy and ill-equipped to even make an attempt to court Ozzie Washington, as much as he wanted to. Life in an orphanage after his father had run off and his mother had died, then the army at fourteen, had promised him no childhood and no way to learn about the finer things.

Years had passed. The press of hospital work, the constant turmoil of fighting, and vast distances had meant no furloughs. The relative isolation of hospital life, and his neither-fish-nor-fowl rank as hospital steward, left him dangling in the vast gulf between enlisted society and the officer corps.

He belonged nowhere and to no one, and the sad fact chafed him raw. He was too shy to speak to Ozzie Washington of anything beyond commonplaces. He, Colm Callahan, organized man of considerable responsibility, didn't know where to begin.

The ward was still shrouded in shadow, but Colm needed only one slat of light to assess his patients. He stood at the foot of the avulsed ankle's bed, amused to see Ozzie's careful handwriting—a contrast to his almost-doctor scrawl—listing each hour she had looked at the man and his condition.

My dear Ozzie, you are nearly as precise as I am, he thought. Private Henry slumbered on, just the way Colm wanted to find him at five o'clock before Reveille.

Private Jones was a different matter, tossing his head from side to side, the portrait of early-morning discomfort that Colm always associated with burns, his least-favorite injury. The soldier wasn't quite awake yet, so the hospital steward pressed his hand on the private's forehead. In a few minutes, he slept again. Funny how just a touch could calm. Some imp sitting on his shoulder suggested that he try touching Ozzie to see what happened. The thought made him roll his eyes.

As he sat with the private, thinking he might have to debride the burn when the light was better, Colm glanced toward Lysander Locke. The actor watched him with what appeared to be considerable interest. When Private Jones drifted deeper into sleep, he tiptoed to Lysander Locke's bed and sat down. After a whispered conversation—at least as quiet as a man with vocal pipes like an actor could whisper—and a moment with the bedpan, Lysander appeared disposed to talk.

"She took good care of me. Uh, sergeant?"

"No. Just Steward, or you may call me Callahan. Captain Dilworth does."

"No first name?"

"Not in the US Army." It was early in the morning; maybe Colm could be forgiven for wishful thinking. "I can't recall the last time anyone used my first name."

He didn't say so for the actor to frown and feel sorry for him, but Mr. Locke did look touched at his pronouncement.

"That's wrong, my boy. What does Miss Washington call you?"

He shrugged, glad that the gloom of early morning hid his blush, if the warmth of his face was any indicator. He thought about it, and suddenly realized that he had a nickname with Ozzie alone, their private name. "She calls me Suh. I told her I wasn't a gentleman and shouldn't be addressed as Sir, but that's what she calls me."

"I like it."

"So do I."

There. He had said enough. His failure at doing what probably eighty percent of the population did by finding a mate was his problem, and not one to share with a bedridden, broken-down actor. He made as if to rise, but Mr. Locke put out his hand. Colm sat down. There was no reason for the man to take an interest in him, but that was what he appeared to do. Right or wrong, Colm couldn't deny feeling flattered.

Lysander Locke leaned forward like a conspirator, so Colm did too.

"Did you know that her real name is Audra?" He didn't. Audra. *Audra*. The name was just exotic enough to match her olive skin and beautiful eyes. He listened as the actor regaled him with information about Ozzie's early life, obviously gleaned during a late-night conversation bearing some resemblance to this early-morning one. None of it was anyone's business, but Colm wanted to know more about the woman sleeping in his bed.

He listened, amused and then touched, to learn of Ozzie's letters to herself. He couldn't remember a time he had ever received correspondence from anyone except the US government, and he admired Ozzie's resourcefulness.

But here was the old gent, clapping his hands softly, demanding attention. "I have an idea! You

could write her a letter. Think how surprised she
would be."

"Oh, I . . ."

Lysander Locke was a professional at riding
over someone else's conversation, if Colm could
call his own mumble actual conversation.
"Think how much you owe her. Just a note of
appreciation."

Colm sat back. It would be a surprise for a
lovely lady, just a note and a penny stamp. "Have
you ever received a letter?" Locke asked.

Colm laughed, then looked around when
Private Jones stirred. "And who would write to
an orphan from Five Points?"

"Surely you made friends in . . . did you fight
in the war?"

"I was only fourteen when I ran away from
St. Agnes," Colm replied. "Enlisted as a drummer boy with the 69th."

"No friends, no comrades in arms?"

It had been a long time; he nearly didn't
falter. "One died at Fredericksburg, and the
other two in a wheat field at Gettysburg."

Thank goodness Private Jones started to
groan; Colm had a perfect excuse to tend to

someone who needed him, and avoid more questions.

"Didn't mean to interrupt your conversation," the private gasped between rapid breaths.

"Easy now," Colm said, happy to devote his attention to something he was familiar with. Letters? He had decided years ago that they were for others.

Colm removed the loose bandage, and the private sucked in his breath. Eyes wide, he stared at the mess that was his own forearm.

"No fears. I'll have you fine in a few days."

And he would. Colm had seen the same worried look on other men with burns. Speaking low and keeping his explanation simple, he told Jones what he would do for the burn to heal properly. "A little morphine will make it easy enough to bear. A few more days, and I'll send you back to the bakehouse."

"To work?" the private asked, uncertainty in his voice.

"To rest. Don't you have quarters off the storeroom? Perfect place to recuperate." Colm rested his hand on the private's shoulder. "Trust me, laddie. I've seen worse."

By the eternal, he had. How curious that he had found his life's vocation in a burning aid station on the second day at Gettysburg. After his commanding officer ordered him to beat retreat through the wheat field, then sank to his knees with a minié ball between his eyes, Colm had done the sensible thing. He beat retreat as ordered, then unhooked his drum and left it there in the wheat field. He took up his other duty as stretcher-bearer and carried out a wounded lieutenant, only to have him burn to death when the nearest aid station took a direct hit from a cannonball. The ether exploded into fireballs, and Colm dragged out the wounded, his own hair singed and stinking.

He went back in, and that made all the difference. When the battle ended two days later, he could debride burns, hold retractors, and throw in a simple suture. He never went back to find his drum, and no one in the Irish Brigade complained.

"Steward?"

Startled, he looked down at his patient. "Sorry, I was doing some rare remembering." He patted the man. "Can you rest now?"

The private obediently did as he was bid. Colm looked back to see Lysander Locke's eyes on him, maybe with admiration in them. With a sigh borne of too little sleep and more recollection than he wanted, Colm again sat beside the actor's bed. To his chagrin, Lysander Locke had not lost the thread of their whispered conversation.

"Well done, Callahan. Do I gather that you have never received a letter either?"

"You gather right, except for memos from the Medical Department."

Colm started to say something else equally inane, but he sniffed the air instead. Good Gadfreys, was that sausage? He couldn't imagine anything less suitable for a low diet, but since Captain Dilworth was not there to enforce the prescribed nutrition for sick men, he, Colm Callahan, was not about to quibble.

"I think I'll check on breakfast," he said to the ward at large. He rose, but Lysander took his hand and tugged it.

"I think you should surprise her with a letter." He gave Colm a calculating look. "Even a shy man can write a letter."

Colm smiled at his patient—Mary and Joseph, but Locke was nosy—and sauntered down the hall to the kitchen.

With the same concentration that he devoted to medical matters, Ozzie was subduing a rank of fat sausages.

"Where in the world did you find those?" he asked by way of greeting.

She pointed to the ice chest. "You should inventory that sometime."

She wore a different dress, and had tried to curb the exuberance of her hair, tying back the mass of curls with a bit of elastic midway up the back of her head. The effect, while disorderly, struck him as charming. He cleared his throat, and screwed up his courage—a different kind of courage than what he had shown on the night-time field at Fredericksburg, or the Gettysburg aid station.

"I owe you a thousand thanks," he said.

She turned around with a smile. "You need me," she said simply, then immediately returned her attention to the sausage, which made him suspect she was shy too.

Perhaps putting trust where she should not, Audra handed Colm the long fork and told him to keep turning the sausage. Meanwhile, she prepared oatmeal and stirred it, standing close to him because it wasn't a large kitchen range.

Audra stopped. Her face was warm, surely from the steam spiraling off the porridge. She took a step away from Colm Callahan, who stared with fierce concentration at the sausages.

When the porridge was subdued into the occasional glop glop, Audra set it at the back of the range and found some brown paper so Colm could spear out the sausages to drain them.

"You sleep all right?" he asked.

"Never better. Except . . ."

"It's a lumpy bed," he said, apologizing for his mattress.

"It's not that. The lumps are in the right places." She transferred the porridge to individual bowls and sugared it well, wondering why she couldn't leave well enough alone and say nothing more.

But he was looking at her, curious and interested. "Colm, I mean Suh, why does your house smell of camphor? It's all over your pillow."

She put her hands to her face, amazed she had mentioned something as intimate as a man's pillow. *You are merely curious*, she reminded herself. "I . . . I sniffed it on you yesterday, Suh."

The range must have been hotter than she thought, because Colm was red-faced too. At least that much color would never show on *her* face.

He chuckled then, apparently deciding not to be embarrassed. "It's this, Audra: I know it's silly after all these years, but the smell of blood makes me queasy. When the bugle summoned me to the ambulance yesterday, I didn't know what I would find, so I dabbed camphor on my upper lip. I can't smell anything else with camphor there. D'ye mind?"

She shook her head. "I just wondered why." She opened her mouth and closed it, wondering why she was turning so nosy.

"Go ahead," he said.

"You called me Audra." There, she said it. Audra waited to feel nervous or embarrassed, but she did not. Maybe she could tell this man anything.

He gave her the kindest expression, even though his face flamed now. "Blame Lysander

Locke." The lilt to his voice was more pro-
nounced, as though he was conscious of every
word he spoke to her. "What did he do but tell
me all about you this morning, how . . . how you
were beaten when you told that little girl your
name was Audra and not Ozzie."

"I've never told anyone before," she murmured, wondering what it was about the actor
that drew out her secrets. Maybe it had been the
late hour. "No one wants to hear such things."

He continued to look at her, measuring her
in some way. "It's no shame," he said finally.

To her amazement, he turned around and
pulled his woolen shirt out of his trousers and
lifted it high enough to show wicked-looking
scars on his back. "I was not the most obedient
orphan at Saint Agnes," he said, as he tucked his
shirt in again. "You're not the only one, Audra.
Why us?"

Shocked, she willed herself to calm, with no
idea how to reply. There was no need to say anything. Mumbling something about checking on
the corpse in the dead house, Colm hurried from
the kitchen.

Her mind in turmoil over what had just happened, Audra served breakfast silently.

Serving, always serving, she thought, distressed with herself at time a-wasting. For the first moment in her parched life, she allowed herself to think of fixing breakfast for just one man, of eating with him, and discussing this and that, as she had seen the Chambers do for years. She knew she wanted those things, but Colm had to make the move. It wasn't something women did, and certainly not maids of color.

She shook her head when Lysander requested that she visit with him, and retreated to the kitchen. She banged the dishes around, blaming them for her misery. She took out her irritation on herself—over the shy hospital steward she loved, with the whole unfair universe—by sweeping the floor with impressive vigor.

"Stop it, Audra," she muttered, and leaned the broom against the wall.

"Beg pardon?"

Suh stood in the doorway.

"I was talking to myself," she said, monumentally dissatisfied with herself.

"Sounded more like a rare scold," he replied with a half-smile. He cleared his throat, and the now-familiar blush rose up his neck from his uniform collar. "Audra, I'm sorry I pulled up my shirt like that. Where have my manners gone?"

Tears filled her eyes. "Maybe I needed reminding that mine was not the only hard life."

"That's not why I did it," he said, coming closer. "I wanted you to see that you and I are not so different. Neither of us had a childhood. I know you're tired, but please watch our patients. I have to embalm that poor coachman." He left, even though the camphor lingered in the room.

Audra dabbed her eyes and returned to the ward, skipping Private Henry, because two of his bunkies must have sneaked away from a work detail to visit the sick and afflicted.

Private Jones lay staring at his bandaged arm, chewing on his lip. Audra sat beside his bed. "You'll have a scar, but that's all," she assured him.

"I have a sweetheart . . ."

"She'll still love you," Audra teased.

He shook his head. "Bet you never met such a coward."

"Burns are difficult." She paused, then had to ask, "Do you get many letters from her?"

He grinned, looking happy for the first time since his arrival. "Every week, without fail. In fact . . ." He glanced over at the party on Private Henry's bed. "Could one of you miscreants go to the post office to see if I have a letter?"

One of the "miscreants" gave him a friendly thumbs up, stood, and sauntered out the door. He was back in ten minutes, waving two letters. He dropped one in Private Jones's lap, and handed the other to Audra, along with a folded note.

"Mrs. Chambers flagged me down and gave this to me," he said. "She had fire in her eyes."

"Oh, dear."

Audra knew the letter was from herself, but she stared at her familiar handwriting a moment, wondering why on earth she had ever thought a fictitious letter from a mother she barely remembered could make up for the real thing.

I have been living in shadows, she thought, tucking the letter in her apron pocket, determined not to look at Private Jones and his real letter.

Mrs. Chambers's familiar scrawl leaped out at her when she unfolded the note. "The Fourth is moving out in four days for Fort Assinniboine, Dakota Territory. Ozzie, we must pack! Only this day and night at the hospital!! That is all!!!"

"No," she said out loud. "I can't go. I *won't* go."

Embarrassed, she looked around. Private Jones was deep in his letter, and someone in Private Henry's traveling circus had broken out a deck of cards. His face placid, his eyes kind, Lysander Locke watched her. She was on her feet even before he gestured to her. She sat down and handed him the note.

He read it and handed it back. "Regiments move around all the time, Miss Washington."

"Yes, but—"

"You'll make new friends there." He folded his hands on his belly. "I always do when I travel from theatre to theatre."

"But I don't want to leave."

"Put away the cards, lads, or I'll put you on report. Faith, now, who's leaving?"

She couldn't help her tears at Colm's familiar voice. Quiet on his feet, his eyes exhausted, he stood by Private Jones's bed, rolling down his sleeves.

"I'm leaving," she said, handing him the note as she leaped up and ran into the hall. She looked around. There was nowhere for her to go. Colm had to sleep, and she had promised to stay. She hurried up the stairs and sat down on the top tread. For years she had worked and moved with no complaints, but now it was too much. She put her head on her knees, wishing to be somewhere else, but desperately wanting to stay right here at Fort Laramie.

Why had she ever offered to help Colm Callahan? All she had done was discover just how much she loved him, and how impossible that was. The man was shy, and she was a woman of color. She shivered against the knowledge that nothing would ever change in her life. Was this freedom?

"It's too much, isn't it?"

She looked down the stairs to see Colm looking up.

"I'm just tired," she told him. That was no lie. She would never tell him how she had tossed about last night, teased by the odor of camphor, wondering how long it was possible to love a person before he could be decently forgotten.

There now, Audra, he has enough to do without worrying about you, she scolded herself. Brace up. When she thought she could, she stood up. Colm was so tired, he looked like he was swaying on his feet. He didn't need her drama. It was time to give her greatest performance.

"You're the one who has had too much to bear," she said, keeping her tone light. "It's your turn to sleep, or . . . or . . ." She laughed and nearly convinced herself. "Or you'll end up in the dead house."

"It won't come to that, but I could use a nap," he admitted, even though the worried look didn't leave his face.

"A nap of about five hours," she insisted.

"All right, all right."

Silent, she walked down the hall with him as he reeled off instructions.

Check: the sergeant of the guard was sending a wagon to take the coffined stagecoach driver to the fort cemetery.

"We haven't heard from the Shy-Dead office yet, so we'll bury him on the end, where they can retrieve him, if need be."

Check: Private Henry was released to ride in the same wagon, and park his bones back in the barracks. "I'll check him tonight. He's with the Fourth, so he'll be packing soon too."

Check: He would take a good look at Private Jones's forearm, decide whether to debride the burn, then send him on his way rejoicing tomorrow.

Check: After that, Lysander Locke would be their only patient, and little trouble. Just this one night more, and he'd release her to the Chambers again. "If the hospital matron still isn't spry, I can get one of the barracks cooks to send us what little Mr. Locke and I will need."

Check: Captain Dilworth would be back in two days, according to the telegram remembered at last by one of Private Henry's partygoers. "If I were a wagering man, I'd bet that nothing at all will happen after he returns."

Then he ran out of steam. "I'm going to sleep, Audra."

"No lunch?"

"Later." A wave of his hand and click, the door to Captain Dilworth's office closed.

Working silently, her jaw clenched against tears, Audra made vegetable soup and sandwiches from leftover sausage for the patients, and for Private Henry's friends too. Lunch was followed in short order by the arrival of the sergeant of the guard and his minions. The coffin left the dead house, taking Private Henry too, perched on the coffin with a pair of crutches and looking more

91

cheerful than when he'd arrived a day ago. He even blew her a kiss, which demanded a smile, however forced.

Private Jones slept the sleep of the blissfully content, letter in hand, so Audra could not ignore Lysander Locke any more. She sat beside him at last, content at least to rest her feet.

When she thought she could look at him, she gave her attention to the actor, wanting to hate him, because he had told Colm Callahan what she had said. She had bared her soul to an actor, of all people, telling him her real name, of the letters from her mother, of her dreams about a clothing shop in Cheyenne.

But she was too generous of heart to be angry with the old busybody. All she saw when she looked at him was a shabby man down on his luck, heading to what couldn't be a good venue for Shakespeare in Deadwood. He was at the end of his career, and it didn't look sanguine. She realized with a tug at her heart that she was looking at herself in thirty years, and probably Colm Callahan too. Alone.

"Mr. Locke, why have you never married?" she asked. "It's the man who does the asking, so you have the advantage. Was there never a pretty actress?"

"Plenty of those," he said, reminiscence in his eyes. "My dear, I gave all for the theatre, and the theatre is a jealous mistress."

"Will you be lonely later?"

He looked her in the eyes. "No lonelier than you, Miss Audra Washington."

They sat together through the afternoon, Audra knitting a pair of socks for the actor because she feared he had no others. Her dusty heart began to heal a bit as, using different voices, he read *A Midsummer Night's Dream* to her and Private Jones. It was a lovely performance, something to treasure in her heart from Fort Laramie. She wondered how much longer the Grand Old Dame near the junction of the Platte and the Laramie would be around, because the frontier was closing. Everything was changing, and she was helpless before circumstance. She even tucked away the dream of her own dress shop in Cheyenne, because she was too tired to make any more effort.

She prepared more flapjacks and eggs for supper and was finishing the dishes when she heard the door to Captain Dilworth's office open. She thought Colm might come into the kitchen, but she heard his footsteps on the stairs. When he came down, he looked in the kitchen.

"I saved some for you."

"You are a peach, Audra," he told her. "I'll eat after I give these crutches to our actor to practice with. I can't do anything else for him, and there is a stage leaving for Deadwood tomorrow morning."

"I'm worried about him," she said. *And about me. Oh, yes, me*, she wanted to add.

"I needn't do any more for him here. He's ready to go." He brightened up. "And now, my dear Miss Washington, you have earned a good night's rest."

Colm did not see Audra in the morning. Still complaining loudly, the hospital matron puffed her way up the hill and reestablished ownership of the kitchen. Private Jones had been a total stoic as Colm tweezed away bits of burned skin, dabbed saline solution, and wrapped the burn in damp gauze. He knew his handiwork was equal to or better than anything Captain Dilworth could do. From a determined drummer boy in a burning aid station at Gettysburg to a competent hospital steward had been the education of nearly twenty years. He knew he could pass the state medical examination in Wyoming Territory, and he liked the high plains.

It's time, he thought. *No more reenlistments.* Mine company doctor, Indian agency doctor, railroad doctor, small-town doctor—he could choose.

After sick call, Colm sent Private Jones on his way, aided by the other baker's assistant and bolstered by Colm's promise to visit twice a day to change his dressing.

Quietly competent in all things, he arranged for a horse and buggy to take Lysander Locke, Shakespeare tragedian of Drury Lane, Broadway, Denver, and Deadwood, to the Rustic Hotel down on the flats. He needed no urging to accompany the old toot.

They hadn't long to wait. They sat together in companionable silence, both of them with their faces raised to the morning sun. Soon August would become September, and all bets would be off as winter peered around the corner. By cold weather, the Fourth would be shivering in drafty barracks at Fort Assinniboine.

Maybe I'll set up practice in Green River, Colm thought. *It's an ugly town, but even ugly towns need physicians.*

He glanced at Lysander Locke, worried for him. "I owe you such a debt," he said, as the Shy-Dead stage came into view. "Could I . . . could I loan you some money? I'm worried that Deadwood won't—"

"Stuff and nonsense," Lysander Locke interrupted. "Actors always land on their feet." He chuckled as he looked down at his plaster cast, new that morning and whittled down to walking size. "Shake my hand, boy, and do what you promised."

Colm took his time writing the perfect letter to Audra Washington. Maybe there was enough of the Irish rascal inherited from his scamp of a father to make it easy to declare himself to the loveliest, best woman he knew. He hadn't enough courage to ask her in person, but he surely wasn't the first man in the universe who ever proposed via the US mail.

The hospital was blissfully empty, tidied just so, with every bed sheet squared away, pillowcases creaseless, and floors swept. After the matron left, he bathed in the fort's only actual bathing room, soaking and thinking. That night, he slept like a virtuous man in his lumpy bed.

In the morning, he put on his best uniform and left a note on Captain Dilworth's desk, informing him that he was not planning to reenlist in September. He had done his duty well enough.

He ambled down to the Rustic Hotel when the stage came in, thinking that Captain and Mrs. Dilworth might need some help with their luggage. They did. He smiled to see that Mrs. Dilworth had two hatboxes she hadn't left with, and she wore a smart new traveling coat.

They hitched a ride with the mail cart, which let them off in front of the surgeon's quarters.

"I suppose the Fourth is packed and ready," Captain Dilworth said.

"Leaving tomorrow, sir."

Since he had been so helpful, Captain Dilworth invited Colm inside. Over malt whiskey that made Mrs. Dilworth frown, Colm described his patients, saving the best for last.

"We even had an old, run-down actor on his way to Deadwood. Broke a leg, but we didn't shoot him."

Funny how malt whiskey loosened his tongue.

"Name of . . . ?" the post surgeon prompted.

"Lysander Locke, Shakespeare tragedian," Colm declared, striking a little pose.

Captain Dilworth gaped at him. "Holy Hannah, you're joking."

"Who would joke about someone named Lysander Locke?"

Captain Dilworth started to laugh. He leaned back and howled at the ceiling while Colm stared at him, suddenly sober.

"Run-down old actor?" Dilworth said when he could speak. "*The* Lysander Locke?"

"Aye, captain," Colm said, smelling a rat.

"To Deadwood, you say? That I can understand."

Colm just stared.

The captain must have decided that his hospital steward needed some enlightenment. "Lysander and Abigail Locke and their two sons own the best theatre in San Francisco."

"But he's alone and nearly destitute!"

"Hardly. He's a rich man with a talented family! They have performed before Queen Victoria, I hear, and a president or two."

"But he was shabby and going to Deadwood," Colm insisted.

The captain leaned forward and whispered, so any road agents within forty miles wouldn't hear him. "He owns a gold mine there called The Merchant of Venice. He was probably just checking on his business interests. Apparently he is eccentric that way."

"How in the world do you know all this?" Colm burst out.

"Mrs. Dilworth reads all the gossip in *Frank Leslie's Illustrated Weekly.*"

Colm wasn't a man to surrender without a fight. "He told us—Audra Washington and me—that he had no family, and he led us to think that he was one step from ruin."

"Callahan, he's an actor," Captain Dilworth said, his eyes lively.

Colm sat back as understanding washed over him. *And he has convinced me to be brave and propose to the woman I love*, he thought. *He preyed on my sympathy until I knew I didn't want to be a*

*lonely man like him. The old rip! He probably did
the same thing with Audra.*

He had one more question. "Do you
know . . . Is he really English?"

"Ames, Iowa."

Colm stood. "I've been fair diddled," he said
with a smile. "Excuse me, sir, but I have a letter
to deliver."

It was only a few steps down Officers Row to
the sutler's store and adjoining post office. The
sun was warm, and it was a good day to whistle,
which caused a head or two to turn. He took a
deep breath when he looked in the store and saw
Audra standing there with a letter in hand.

God is good, he thought to himself.

He waited until she walked the few feet into
the adjoining post office, a closet-sized box with
an iron railing. He cleared his throat, and she
turned around.

Wordless, terrified, he held out his letter, the
one with all the love in his heart on two close-
written pages. She took it as she handed him a
letter.

This wouldn't do. He looked at the sutler,
who watched them with some interest.

"Mr. London, is the enlisted canteen open yet?"

"Too early, Steward," he said with a smile.

"Could you . . . could you let me have the key? We'll only be a few minutes."

Mr. London handed it over. Colm took Audra by the arm, but that suddenly wasn't close enough. He put his hand on her waist, and with a sigh, she sort of melted into his side. Mr. London's back was turned, so he kissed her cheek.

The canteen was dark and cool, smelling of stale beer, trapped smoke, and spittoons that needed attention. It was no place to propose, but that was army life. Silent, he sat them both down. Her breath came a little fast, but he didn't think she would hyperventilate. If she did, he could find a paper bag for her to breathe in.

Her fingers shook, but she took out his letter and spread it on her lap. He took out her letter and did the same. He read quickly and let out a deep breath. Maybe it was worth a lifetime's famine to read "beloved," and know he was the one beloved. His clinical mind almost suggested to him that "adore" was over the top, but for once, his heart overruled his brain.

She finished first. "Yes, Suh," was all she said, but it said the earth, moon, planets, and a galaxy or two.

No expert, he kissed Audra Washington. She kissed back, no expert either. They were both in good health; they had years to improve.

In the cool of the enlisted men's canteen, he told her of his plans to take the medical boards in the fall, and to find a little town that needed him in a territory with nothing but little towns. "I've saved for years. I can set up an office."

"I've saved too. We can have a house with running water."

She was on his lap then, both arms around him, head pressed to his chest, where his heart was doing things that, in a big city, would have landed him in a cardiac ward.

"I wish . . . I wish we could tell that dear old man. Would you mind . . . If Deadwood doesn't work out for Mr. Locke, we could find a place for him with us, couldn't we?"

"Certainly."

Lysander Locke could wait. Colm Callahan wanted to kiss Audra Washington a few more times before Mr. London got curious. Maybe they could honeymoon in Deadwood. Colm did like to check up on his discharged patients.

A Season for Heroes

*E*zra Freeman died yesterday. I don't usually read the obituaries; at least I didn't until after Pearl Harbor. With four grandsons in the service now and one of them based in the Solomons and missing over a place called Rabaul, or some such thing, I generally turn to the obituaries after the front page and the editorials.

There it was, right at the bottom of the column, in such small print that I had to hold the paper out at arm's length . . . *Ezra Freeman*. There was no date of birth listed, probably because even Ezra hadn't known that, but it did mention there were no surviving relatives and that the deceased had been a veteran of the Indian Wars.

When I thought about Ezra Freeman, I ended up thinking about Mother and Father. Still carrying the newspaper, I went into my bedroom and looked at the picture of Mother and Father and D Company hanging on the wall next to the window. It was taken just before Father was promoted and bumped up to a desk job in San Antonio, so he is still leaning on a cane in the picture. Mother is sitting on a bench holding quite a small baby, and, next to her, his shoulders thrown back and his boots together, is Sergeant Ezra Freeman.

The picture was taken at Fort Bowie, Arizona Territory. I was ten or eleven then, and that memory was one of the first that really stuck in my mind. It was where Father nearly got killed, my little brother was born, and I discovered a few things about love.

My mother was what people call lace-curtain Irish. She was born Kathleen Mary Flynn. Her father owned a successful brewery in upstate New York, and Mother was educated at a convent, where she learned to speak French and make lace. She never owned up to learning anything else there, although she wrote with a fine copperplate hand and did a lot of reading when

Father was campaigning. The nuns taught her good manners and how to pour tea the right way. Father could always make her flare up by winking at her and saying in his broadest brogue, "What'll ye hev to dhrink now, Kate Flynn?"

She had beautiful red hair that curled every which way. Little springs of it were forever popping out of the bun she wore low on her neck. She had a sprinkling of light brown freckles that always mystified the Indians. I remember the time an old San Carlos Apache stopped us as we were walking down Tucson's main street. He spoke to Father in Apache. Father answered him, and we could see he was trying to keep a straight face.

We pounced on him after the Indian nodded, gave Mother a searching look, and walked away.

"What did he say, Father, what did he say?"

Father shook his head and herded us around the corner where he leaned against the wall and laughed silently until tears shone on his eyelashes. Mother got exasperated.

"What *did* he say, John?"

"Oh, Kate Flynn," he wheezed and gasped, "he wanted to know . . . Oh, sweet merciful me . . ." He went off in another quiet spasm.

"John!" Mother didn't approve of even wooden swearing, as she called it (which made garrison life a trial for her at times).

"Sorry, Kathleen." Father looked at her and winked. I could feel Mother stiffening up. "He wanted to know if you had those little brown dots all over."

We children screamed with laughter. Mother blushed. A lesser Victorian lady would have swooned, I suppose, but Tucson's streets were dusty then, and Father was laughing too hard to catch her on the way down.

Mother and Father met after Father's third summer at West Point. He had been visiting friends of his family in Buffalo, and Mother had been a guest of one of the daughters. They had spent a week in each other's company; then Mother had gone back to the convent. They corresponded on the sly for several months. Father proposed during Christmas furlough. They were married after graduation in June.

There had been serious objections on both sides of the family. Papa Flynn made Father promise to raise any children as Catholics, and Grandpa Stokes wanted to be reassured that he and Grandma wouldn't be obliged to call on the Flynns too often.

Father agreed to everything, and he would have raised us as Catholics, except that we seldom saw a priest out on the plains. Besides, Mother wasn't a very efficient daughter of the Church. I think she figured she'd had enough, what with daily Mass at the convent for six years straight. In spite of that, she always kept her little ebony-and-silver rosary in her top drawer under her handkerchiefs, and I only saw her fingering it once.

I don't remember what my father looked like in those early years. I do remember that he wasn't too tall (few of the horse soldiers were), and that the other officers called him Handsome Johnny. Mother generally called him "the Captain" when we were around. "The Captain says you should do this, Janey," or "Take the Captain's paper to him, Gerald." When he was promoted, she called him "the Major," and the last name before he died was "the Colonel." Fifteen years later, just before she died, Mother had started over and was calling him "the Lieutenant" again.

I was born about a year after they were married. Pete came along two years later at Fort Sill, and Gerald was born at Fort Robinson near the Black Hills.

When I was ten, we were assigned to Fort Bowie, Arizona Territory. That was in the fall of 1881, more than sixty years ago. Father commanded D Company of the Tenth Cavalry (the Ninth and Tenth Cavalry were composed entirely of Negro enlisted men, serving under white officers). The Indians called them Buffalo Soldiers, I suppose because their kinky black hair reminded them of the hair of a buffalo. Father always swore they were the best troops in the whole US Army and said he was proud to serve with them, even though some of his brother officers considered such duty a penance.

My favorite memory of D Company was listening to them ride into Fort Bowie after duty in the field. They always came in singing. The only man who couldn't carry a tune was my father. I remember one time right before Christmas when they rode out of Apache Pass singing "Star of the East," Mother came out on the porch to listen, her hand on my shoulder.

D Company had two Negro sergeants. Sergeant Albert Washington was a former slave from Valdosta, Georgia. He was a short, skinny little man who never said very much, maybe because he was married to Clara Washington, who did our washing and sewing and who had the loudest, strongest voice between the Mississippi and the Pacific.

The other sergeant was Ezra Freeman. Ezra wasn't much taller than my father, and he had the biggest hands I ever saw. They fascinated me because he was so black and the palms of his hands were so white.

Ezra had a lovely deep voice that reminded me of chocolate pudding. I loved to hear him call the commands to the troops during Guard Mount, and I loved to watch him sit in his saddle. My father was a good horseman, but he never sat as tall as Ezra Freeman, and Father's shoulders got more and more stooped as the years passed. Not Ezra's. Last time I saw him sitting in his wheelchair, his posture was as good as ever; I think he would have died before he would have leaned forward.

Once I asked Ezra about his childhood. He said that he had been raised on a plantation in South Carolina. At the age of twelve, he and two sisters and his mother and father had been sold at the Savannah auction to help pay off his master's gambling debts. He never saw any of his family again. A planter from Louisiana bought him, and he stayed a field hand until Admiral Farragut steamed up the Mississippi and ended slavery on the lower river. He sometimes spoke a funny kind of pidgin French that made my mother laugh and shake her head.

But she never got too close to Ezra or to any of Father's other troopers. None of the white women of the regiment did, either. Mother never would actually pull her skirts aside when the colored troopers passed, as some of the ladies did, but she had a formality about her in the presence of the Buffalo Soldiers that we weren't accustomed to. At least, she did until the summer of 1882, when we came to owe Ezra Freeman everything.

That was the summer Ignacio and his Apaches left the San Carlos Agency and raided, looted, burned, and captured women and children to sell in Mexico. The troops garrisoned at Bowie knew that Ignacio's activities would touch them soon, and the early part of the summer was spent in refitting and requisitioning supplies and ordnance in preparation for the orders they knew would come.

Mother wasn't receiving any callers that summer. That was how we put it then. Or we might have said that she was "in delicate health." Now, in 1942, we say, "she is expecting," or, "she is in the family way." Back then, that would have been altogether too vulgar and decidedly low class.

Neither of them told us. I just happened to notice Mother one morning when I burst into her room and caught her in her shift. She bulged a little in the front, and I figured we were going to have another baby brother sometime. They seemed to lose interest in having girls after me. She didn't say anything then, and I didn't, either. Later on in the week, when we were polishing silver, she paused, put her hand on her middle, and stared off in space for a few minutes, a slight smile on her face.

At breakfast a few mornings later, Father came right out and asked Mother if she wanted to go home for the summer to have the baby. The railroad had been completed between Bowie and Tucson, and it would be a much less difficult trip.

"Oh, no, I couldn't, John," she replied.

"Why not? I'll probably be gone all summer anyway, and you know the surgeon travels with us." Father wiped the egg juice off his plate with one swipe of his toast and grinned when Mother frowned at him.

"Oh, I just couldn't, John," she repeated, and that was the end of that.

Two weeks later, three of the cavalry companies and two of the infantry were detached from Bowie to look for Ignacio. Mother said her good-byes to Father in their bedroom. As I think of it, few of the wives ever saw their husbands off from the porch, except for Lieutenant Grizzard's wife, and everyone said she was a brassy piece anyway.

We kids followed Father out onto the porch. My little brother Pete wore the battered black felt hat Father always took on campaign, and Gerald lugged out the saber, only to be sent back into the house with the useless thing. Father let me carry out his big Colt revolver, and I remember that it took both hands to carry it.

He took the gun from me and pushed it into his holster. He put his hand on my head and shook it back and forth. Then he knelt down and kissed me on both cheeks.

"Keep an eye on Mother for me, Janey," he said.

I nodded, and he stood up and shook my head again. He plucked the black hat off Pete's head and swatted him lightly with it. He knelt down again, and both Pete and Gerald clung to him.

"Now, you two mind Janey. She's sergeant major."

D Company rode out at the head of the column after Guard Mount, and the corporal who taught school for the garrison's children was kind enough to dismiss us for the day.

Summers are always endless to children, but that summer of 1882 seemed to stretch out like cooling taffy. One month dragged by, and then two, and still the men didn't return. In fact, another company was sent out, and Bowie had only the protection of one understrength company of infantry and the invalids in the infirmary.

The trains stopped running between Bowie and Tucson because of Ignacio and his warriors, and I recall how irritated Mother was when the last installment of a serial in *Frank Leslie's Illustrated Weekly* never showed up. The only mail that got through was official business that the couriers brought in.

But Mother was irritated with many things that summer. She usually didn't show much until the eighth month, but this time she had Clara Washington sew her some new Mother Hubbards before her sixth month. Her ankles were swollen too. I rarely saw Mother's legs, but once I caught her on the back porch one evening with her dress up around her knees.

"Oh, Mama!" was all I said.

It startled her, and she dropped her skirts and tucked her feet under the chair. "Jane, you shouldn't spy on people!" she scolded, and then she smiled when she saw my face. "Oh, I'm sorry, Jane. And don't look so worried. They'll be all right again soon."

Toward the middle of August, we began to hear rumors in the garrison. Ordinarily we just shrugged off rumors, but the men were now quite overdue, and Ignacio hadn't been subdued or chased back across the border. One rumor had the troops halfway across Mexico pursuing Apaches, and another rumor had them in San Diego waiting for a troop train back.

On the eighteenth of August (I remember the date because it was Gerald's fifth birthday), the rumor changed. A couple of reservation Apaches slouched in on their hard-ridden ponies to report a skirmish to the south of us, hard by the Mexican border. Captain Donnelly, B Company, Fourth Infantry, was senior officer of the fort then, and he ignored the whole thing. The Indians weren't students of the truth, and they often confused Mexican and US soldiers.

I mentioned the latest rumor to Mother, who smiled at me and gave me a little shake. I went back outside to play, but I noticed a look in her eyes that hadn't been there before.

Two days later, the troops rode in. They were tired, sunburned, and dirty, and their remounts looked mostly starved. Mother came out on the porch. She leaned on the porch railing and stood on one foot and then the other. I saw that she had taken off her wedding ring and Father's West Point ring that she always wore on her first finger. Her hands looked swollen and tight.

The troops assembled on the parade ground and some of the women and children ran out to them. We looked hard for D Company, but it wasn't there. Mother sat down on the bench under the parlor window.

Several of the officers dismounted and stood talking together. One of them gestured our way, and Mother got up quickly. When Major Connors started walking over to our quarters, she backed into the house and jerked me in with her.

"Listen to me, Jane Elizabeth," she hissed, and her fingers dug into my shoulders until I squirmed in her grasp. "You take their message."

"But Mother," I whined, trying to get out of her grip, "why don't you?"

"It's bad luck," she said and turned and went into the parlor, slamming the door behind her.

Major Connors didn't seem too surprised that Mother wouldn't come out to talk to him. I backed away from him myself because he smelled so awful. "Jane, tell your mother than D Company and A are both a bit overdue but not to worry because we expect them any time."

After he left, I told Mother, but she wouldn't come out of the parlor until suppertime.

Several days passed, and then a week, and still no sign of either company. None of the other officers' wives said anything to Mother about the delay, but several of them paid her morning calls and brought along baked goods.

"Why are they doing this, Mama?" I asked her, after Captain O'Neill's wife left an eggless custard.

Mother murmured something about an early wake. I asked her what she meant, but she shook her head. My brothers and I downed all the cakes and pies, but Mother wouldn't eat any of it.

One night when I couldn't sleep because of the heat, I crept downstairs to get a drink of water from the pump. Mother was sitting on the back porch, rocking slowly in the moonlight. She heard me and closed her fist over something in her lap, but not before I'd seen what it was: the little ebony rosary she kept in her drawer. I could tell by the look in her face that she didn't want me to say anything about it. She rocked, and I sat down near her on the porch steps.

"Mama, what happens if he doesn't come back?" I hadn't really meant to say that; it just came out. She stopped rocking. I thought she might be angry with me, but she wasn't.

"Oh, we'll manage, Jane. It won't be as much fun, but we'll manage."

"Would . . . would we move back east?"

She must not have thought that far, because she was silent a while. "No, I don't think so," she said finally. "I like it out west. So did . . . does . . . your father."

She rocked on in silence, and I could hear, above the creak of the rocking chair, the click of the little ebony beads. I got up to go, and she took my hand.

"You know, Jane, there's one terrible thing about being a woman."

I looked down at her. Her ankles and hands were swollen, her belly stretched tight against the nightgown that usually hung loose on her, and her face was splotched. "What's that, Mama?"

"The waiting, the waiting."

She didn't say anything else, so I went back upstairs and finally fell asleep after the duty guards had called the time from post to post all around the fort.

Another week passed, and still no sign of the companies. The next week began as all the others had. The blue sky was cloudless, and the sun beat down until the whole fort shimmered. Every glance held a mirage.

It was just after Stable Call that I heard the singing. The sound came up faintly, and for a few moments, I wasn't sure I heard anything except the wind and the stable noises to the south of us. But there it was again, and closer. It sounded like "Dry Bones," and that had always been one of Father's favorite songs.

I turned to call Mother, but she was standing in the doorway, her hand shading her eyes as she squinted toward Apache Pass. People popped out of houses all along Officers Row, and the younger children began pointing and then running west past the administration building and the infirmary.

There they were, two columns of blue filing out of the pass, moving slowly. The singing wasn't very loud, and then it died out as the two companies approached the stables. Mother took her hand away from her eyes. "He's not there, Janey," she whispered.

I looked again. I couldn't see Father anywhere. She stood still on the porch and shaded her eyes again. Then she gave a sob and began running.

So many nights in my dreams I've seen my mother running across the parade ground. She was so large and clumsy then, and, as I recall, she was barefoot, but she ran as lightly as a young child, her arms held out in front of her. In my dreams, she runs and runs until I wake up.

I was too startled to follow her at first, and then I saw her run to the back of the column and drop down on her knees by a travois one of the horses was pulling. The animal reared back and then nearly kicked her, but I don't think she even noticed. Her arms were around a man lying on the travois. As I ran closer, I could see him raise his hand slowly and put it on her hair.

I didn't recognize my father at first. His hair was matted with blood, and I thought half his head had been blown away. There was a bloody, yellowish bandage over one eye, and his face was swollen. He turned his head in my direction, and I think he tried to smile, but he only bared his teeth at me, and I stepped back.

I wanted to turn and run, and I didn't see how Mother could stand it. But there she was, her head on his chest. She was saying something to him I couldn't hear, and all the while, he was stroking her hair with that filthy, bruised hand.

I backed up some more and bumped into Ezra Freeman. I tried to turn and run, but he held me there. "Go over to him, Janey," he urged and gave me a push. "He wants you."

I couldn't see how Ezra could interpret the slight movement of Father's hand, but he was pushing me toward the travois. "Pa? Pa?" I could feel tears starting behind my eyelids.

He said something that I couldn't understand because it sounded as if his mouth was full of mashed potatoes. I leaned closer. He smelled of blood, sweat, dirt, and wood smoke. As I bent over him, I could see under the bandage on his face and gasped to see teeth and gums where his cheek should have been.

Mother was kneeling by him, her hand on his splinted leg. She took my hand in her other hand and placed it on his chest. He tried to raise his head, and I leaned closer. I could make out the words "Janey" and "home," but what he was saying was unimportant. All of a sudden I didn't care what he looked like. He was my father, and I loved him.

He must have seen my feelings in my eyes because he lay back again and closed his eye. His hand relaxed and let go of mine. I helped Mother to her feet, and we stood back as two orderlies lifted him off the travois and onto a stretcher. He moaned a little, and Mother bit her lip.

They took him to the infirmary, and Ezra Freeman walked alongside the stretcher, steadying it. Mother would have followed him, but the post surgeon took one look at her and told her to go lie down, because he didn't have time to deliver a baby just then. Mother blushed, and the two of us walked back to our quarters hand in hand.

Mother spent an hour that evening in the infirmary with Father. She came home and reported that he looked a lot better and was asleep. We went upstairs then, and while she tucked Gerald and Pete in bed, I sat on the rag rug by Pete's army cot, and she told us what happened.

"The two companies had separated from the main detachment and after a couple days, they found an Apache rancheria. It was at the bottom of a small canyon near Deer Spring. When they tried to surround it before daybreak, they were pinned down by rifle fire from the rim of the canyon." Mother paused, and I noticed that she had twisted her fingers into the afghan at the foot of Pete's bed.

He sat up. "What happened, Ma? What happened?" He pulled on her arm a little, and his eyes were shining. He had been down at the creek that afternoon and hadn't seen Father yet. The whole thing was still just a story to him.

While the candle on the nightstand burned lower and lower, Mother told how Father had been shot while trying to lead the men back to the horses. He had lain on an exposed rock all morning until Ezra Freeman crawled out and pulled him to safety. The two men had stayed in a mesquite thicket, firing at the Apaches until the sun went down. They withdrew in the dark.

Peter fell asleep then, but Mother went on to say that the men had holed up for several days about sixty miles south of us because they were afraid Father would die if they moved him. When it looked like he would make it, they started slowly for the fort.

Gerald fell asleep then, and as Mother pulled the sheet up around him, she said to me, "I can't understand it, Jane. Everyone else thought the Captain was dead. Why did Sergeant Freeman do it?"

She tucked me in my bed, but I couldn't sleep. Every time I closed my eyes, I kept seeing Father on that travois and the look in Mother's eyes as she knelt by him. I got out of bed and started into Mother's room.

She wasn't there; the bed hadn't even been slept in. I tiptoed down the stairs, stepping over the third tread because it always squeaked. As I groped to the bottom in the dark, I saw the front door open and then close quietly.

I waited a few seconds, then opened it and stood on the porch. Mother was dressed and wrapped in a dark shawl, despite the heat, and walking across the parade ground. She wasn't going toward the infirmary, so I trailed her, skirting around the parade ground and keeping in the shadow of the officers' quarters. I didn't know where she was going, but I had a feeling that she would send me back if she knew I was following her.

She passed the quartermaster's building and the stables, pausing to say something to the private on guard, who saluted her and waved her on. I waited until he had turned and walked into the shadows of the blacksmith shop before I continued.

I could see now that she was heading for Suds Row, where the enlisted men with families lived. Halfway down the row of attached quarters she stopped and knocked on one of the doors. I ducked behind the row until I came to the back of the place where she had knocked. There was a washtub in the yard, and I staggered with it to the window, turned it over, and climbed up.

Ezra lived in the barracks with his company, but Mother must have found out he was visiting Sergeant Jackson Walter of A Company and Jackson's wife, Chloe. Mother and Ezra were standing in the middle of the room. She had taken off her shawl. Freeman offered her the chair he had been sitting in, but she shook her head. I could see Chloe knitting in the rocking chair by the kitchen.

Mother was silent a few moments. "I just wanted to say thank you, Sergeant Freeman," she said finally. Her voice sounded high and thin, like it did after Grandpa Flynn's funeral three years before.

"Oh . . . well . . . I . . . heavens, ma'am, you're welcome," Ezra stammered.

She shrugged her shoulders and held out her hands. "I mean, Sergeant, you didn't even know if he was alive, and you went out there anyway."

He didn't say anything. All I could hear was the click of Chloe's bone needles. I barely heard Mother's next word.

"Why?"

Again that silence. Ezra Freeman turned a little, and I could see his face. His head was down, he had sucked in his lower lip, and he was crying. The light from the kerosene lamp was reflected in his tears, and they shone like diamonds on his black face.

"Well, by the Eternal, ma'am . . . he's the only man I ever served of my own free will." He paused. "And I guess I love him."

Mother put her hands to her face, and I could see her shoulders shaking. Then she raised her head, and I don't think she ever looked more beautiful. "I love him too, Ezra. Maybe for the same reason."

Then she sort of leaned against him, and his arms went around her, and they held onto each other, crying. She was patting him on the back like she did when Father hugged her, and his hand was smoothing down her hair where it curled at the neck.

I am forever grateful that the white ladies and gents of Fort Bowie never saw the two of them together like that, for I am sure they would have been scandalized. As I stood there peeking in the window, I had the most wonderful feeling of being surrounded by love, all kinds of love, and I wanted the moment to last forever.

But the moment passed too soon. They both backed away from each other, and Mother took out a handkerchief from the front of her dress and blew her nose. Ezra fished around in his pocket until he found a red bandanna and wiped his eyes. He sniffed and grinned at the same time.

"Ma'am, I ain't cried since that Emancipation Proclamation."

She smiled at him and put her hand on his arm but didn't say anything. Then she nodded to Chloe, put her shawl around her head again, and turned to the door. "Good night, and thank you again," she said before she went outside.

I jumped off the washtub and ran down the little alley behind the quarters. Staying in the shadows and watching out for the guards, I ran home. I wanted to be home before Mother because I knew she would look in on us before she went to sleep.

She did. She opened the door a crack, and then opened it wider and glided in. I opened my eyes a little and stretched, as if she had just wakened me. She bent down and kissed me, then kissed Gerald and Pete. She closed the door, and soon I heard her getting into bed.

One week later, a couple of troopers from D Company carried Father home on a stretcher. The doctor insisted on putting him in the parlor on the daybed because he didn't want him climbing the stairs.

The post surgeon had done a pretty good job on Father's face. The bandages were off so the air could get at his cheek, which was a crisscross maze of little black sutures. He had lost his left eye and wore a patch over the socket. Later on, he tried to get used to a glass eye but never could get a good fit. He gradually accumulated a cigar box full of glass eyes, and we used them to scare our city cousins and play a kind of lopsided marbles game. His mouth drooped down at one corner and made him look a little sad on one side. None of the other officers called him Handsome Johnny again.

The day after he had been set up in the parlor, Mother went into labor. The post surgeon tried to stop him, but Father climbed the stairs slowly, hand over hand on the railing, and sat by Mother until their third boy was born.

An hour later, the doctor motioned my brothers and me into the room. Mother was lying in the middle of the bed, her red hair spread around the pillow like a fan. Her freckles stood out a little more than usual, but she was smiling. Father sat in an armchair near the bed holding the baby, who had a red face and hair to match.

"What are you going to name him?" I asked, after giving him a good look.

Mother hesitated a moment, then looked over at the baby and Father. "Ezra Freeman Stokes," she replied quietly, her eyes on Father.

He said something to her that I couldn't understand because his face was still swollen. Mother kept her eyes on his and snapped back to him in a low voice that sent shivers down my back. "I don't give a . . . a flea's leap in that hot place what the garrison thinks! He's going to be Ezra Freeman!"

None of us had ever heard Mother come that close to swearing, and Father nearly dropped the baby. That was how Ez got his name. A month later, Father was promoted to major. By the end of the year, he was awarded the Medal of Honor for "meritorious gallantry under fire at Deer Spring." I remember how he pushed that medal around in its plush velvet case, and then closed the box with a click. "I'm not the one who should be getting this," he murmured. No one could ever prevail upon him to wear it. Even when he was laid out in his coffin years later, with his full dress uniform and all his medals, I never saw that one.

With his promotion, Father was transferred to the Third Cavalry, a white regiment. We didn't see Ezra Freeman after that and never did correspond with him because he couldn't read or write. Somehow we always heard about him from the other officers and men of D Company, and every year, at Christmas, Mother sent him a dried apple fruitcake and socks she had knitted. We knew when he retired twenty-five years later and learned in 1915 that he had entered the Old Soldiers' Home in Los Angeles.

Before Father's stroke, he paid him one visit there. I remembered that it was 1919, and Father went to tell him that Captain Ezra F. Stokes had died in France of Spanish influenza.

"You know, Janey," he told me after that visit, "Ez may have been my son, but I ended up comforting Sergeant Freeman. I almost wish I hadn't told him."

After Father passed away, Mother paid Ezra a yearly visit. She insisted on going alone on the train up from San Diego, but when her eyesight began to fade, she finally relented and let me come with her once. As it turned out, it was her last trip. I think she knew.

Sergeant Freeman was in a wheelchair by then, and after giving me a nod and telling me to wait there, Mother pushed Ezra down the sidewalk to a little patio under the trees. She sat next to him on the bench, and they talked together. After about half an hour, she took an object out of her purse, leaned toward Ezra, and put something on the front of his robe. I could tell that Ezra was protesting. He tried to push her hands away, but she went ahead and put something on him. It flashed in the sunlight, but I was too far away to make out what it was.

She took a handkerchief out of her pocket and wiped his eyes. She sat down again beside him, and they sat there together until his head nodded forward, and he fell asleep. She wheeled him back to the far entrance of the building, and I never had a chance to say goodbye.

She was silent on the trip home. After we got to the house, she said, "Jane, I feel tired," and went to bed. She drifted in and out of sleep for the next two days, and then she died.

After the funeral, I was going through her things when I came across the plush velvet case containing the Medal of Honor Father had been awarded for Deer Spring. I snapped it open but the medal was gone. I knew where it went.

And now Ezra's dead.

Well. I can see I've spent more time on this than I intended. I hear the postman's whistle outside. I hope there's a letter from my daughter, Ann. It's her oldest boy, Steve, who has been missing over Rabaul for more than a month now. I don't suppose I can give her much comfort, but I can tell her something about waiting.

Take a Memo

Not for the first time, Corporal of the Day Theodore Sheppard wondered why someone, likely an officer, had decreed the officer of the day building be constructed so far away from the commanding officer's quarters. The morning had proved quiet, so he leaned in unsoldierly fashion against the doorframe, looking south.

Granted, there were many reasons why a distant figure would be striding in front of Officers Row, headed toward him. Ted could tell the figure getting closer and closer walked with more purpose than someone out for a mere stroll. As soon as he saw a piece of paper in the soldier's hand, he knew the matter would soon involve him. Ted straightened up and then relaxed again when he discerned no gold bars on shoulders.

Whatever the concern, the corporal of the day hoped for an outdoor assignment. Each warm and sunny August day at Fort Buford in Dakota Territory was a jewel attached to the crown of summer, which would soon turn—and quickly—into howling winds, endless snow, and temperatures registering so low in the bulb that he hadn't the courage to look at the infernal glass tube.

The only thing better than time spent outdoors now would be a summons to the post hospital. Corporal Sheppard didn't care for the sickbed more than any other healthy man, but the hospital held an attraction that almost made him want to whine about fictitious illness at sick call—Millie Drummond.

A higher-than-normal round of catarrh, pleurisy, and bronchitis in January year of our Lord 1880 had compelled the post surgeon to search for an assistant hospital matron. He had found one in Millie, after promising her mother that Millie wouldn't be called upon to bathe soldiers, or help the surgeon beyond dealing with the more socially acceptable parts of a person for an unmarried woman to tend.

Even that wasn't good enough for Millie's father, first sergeant in A Company, Seventh Infantry, who had told Ted all this one night when both of them were filling in for others in the guardhouse. "She's no delicate girl, is Millie," Angus Drummond had said in his Lowland Scots brogue. "She's a girl, though, and doesn't need to see men's parts yet. She's spending her time in the kitchen. Her mother and I insisted."

Ted could have argued that Millie was more than a girl. He knew she was almost twenty, and back from several years of schooling in Chatfield, Minnesota, where other Drummonds had settled. She was red of hair like her father, but slightly tan of cheek like her mother, who had not-so-distant relatives among the Minnesota Leech Lake Ojibwe. Oh, and her brown eyes were deep pools of possibility. Ted reasoned that to a father, Millie would always be a little girl.

The corporal knew several of his equals in rank and one or two sergeants had proposed to Millie. Each time he heard of this, Ted prepared to bow to the inevitable. So far, no one had convinced Millie Drummond to leave the parental nest.

He had spent many a night lying in his solitary room—one unimaginably wonderful benefit of corporal status—wondering what he could possibly offer Miss Drummond. He was tall and sturdy, as a good corporal of infantry should be, and well on his way to advancement to sergeant. He had all his hair and all his teeth and had recently been selected as Fort Buford's superior marksman. He subscribed to the *Indiana Herald* in his hometown of Huntington, and frequently checked out books from the post library. He was temperate in his habits and neither smoked nor chewed. Whether he was a lover or not was probably open to dispute, considering the paucity of opportunity in Dakota Territory. He knew he had the confidence; time would tell.

He straightened up again to receive the private's salute and the hand off of memo. Another salute followed, and he went inside to read the message.

Ted Sheppard's heart took a nosedive. He was to report immediately to the commanding officer's house for an assignment that could not wait. He left a note on his desk, and accompanied the private, who waited for him outside the small building.

"The CO was in a rare pelter," the private commented.

"What's the emergency?" Ted asked, wanting as much warning as he could muster.

"The hospital is in big trouble," was all the man would say, but his grin was impossible to ignore.

The grin suggested it wasn't Lakota—Sitting Bull's shabby band had been slipping back across the Canadian border for months—and probably not road agents. Something was brewing at the hospital. Ted thought briefly of Millie and trusted no harm had come to her. He wasn't about to ask the private anything so personal. A man had to hold his cards pretty close to his vest at Fort Buford, an isolated post where any hint of rumor was chewed over like an old bone.

Suddenly, Ted understood the private's grin. Grazing between two of the officers' duplexes were three cows: two Holsteins and a Jersey, the sum total of the hospital's herd, allowed because invalids needed nourishment not ordinarily found in a typical soldier's diet.

From lifelong habit, the corporal of the guard looked down and narrowly avoided contact with cow flop. This was no typical cow flop, but the kind that comes from cows clandestinely grazing in deeper grass far superior to their regular diet of hay. Too bad the cows didn't understand that one of Major Brotherton's great prides was a grassy parade ground. Unmindful of the official storm of memos descending upon them, the hospital cows grazed with the unconcerned nonchalance that bovines had cultivated through centuries of domesticity.

"Just how angry is he?" Ted asked the private, who also watched where he walked.

"Red of face, but he's not swearing yet," the private answered. He chuckled. "Better you than me, Corporal Sheppard."

Corporal Sheppard eyed the cows for a long minute. His gaze softened to see Millie Drummond standing between the double row of officers' quarters, hands on her hips. Happy to postpone a visit with an incensed field officer, Ted walked toward her.

"They escaped," she said. "I don't think I can get them back by myself."

"I'll help you, Miss Drummond," Ted told her, wondering at the workings of fate. "First I must see what the major has to say."

"It won't be pretty. This same thing happened two weeks ago when your company was on the mail run to Bismarck," she told him, coming closer and watching her steps too. "He even issued a special order."

Flattered that Millie Drummond even knew his company had served as escort to the steamboat making the twice-monthly mail run to Bismarck, Ted stood beside the pretty lass, noting her height, or lack thereof, and nice shape. He forced his mind back to the cows, one of which had lowered herself with a soft *oof!* to begin chewing her cud. Another cow squirted, and the remaining cow grazed. This was no romantic scene, but Ted knew from long experience in the US Army to take the good times when a man found them. He chose to overlook the cow fragrance and admired Millie's dark hair in its single loose braid.

Discipline overrode desire all too soon to please the corporal. He gave Millie a little one-finger salute, which she returned with a shy smile, and crossed the row to the major's quarters, where the man also maintained his office.

Major Brotherton wasn't precisely tapping his foot impatiently on his porch, but he did mutter something about corporals of the guard who took their sweet time. Ted executed a much smarter salute than the one he gave Millie and stood at rigid attention.

"You can see the problem, corporal," his commanding officer said, with no little sarcasm. "Smell it too, I'll wager."

"Yes, sir. You would like me to return these cows to their grazing area behind the hospital, sir?"

"Oh, no. Impound them in the quartermaster corral, pursuant to Order Number Twenty-four, then deliver this memo to the post surgeon." The major held out a dispatch, folded twice lengthwise, one of many he probably sent and received each week. Brotherton's current temporary adjutant—a poor, long-suffering second lieutenant—did double duty with his own company, and had less time than usual to do the major's dirty work. The man was nowhere in sight and Corporal Sheppard could scarcely fault him.

Corporal Sheppard took the memo and saluted. "Very well, sir. Should I wait for a reply, sir?"

"No. I am certain this will bring the post surgeon here in fine feather."

Sheppard saluted and turned to leave, but Major Brotherton called him back. "When you return to the officer of the guard building, get four inmates to police these grounds."

"Yes, sir!"

Before he enlisted in the post-Civil War army and left to find adventure on the northern plains, Ted Sheppard had been an Indiana farm boy himself. He had led many a cow from the pasture to the milking barn, in fact, too many. Joining the army had come as a relief.

Here he was, herding cows again, but this time with the assistance—or at least the concern—of a pretty girl he yearned to know better. He kicked the Jersey to her feet and was rewarded with a wounded look from both pairs of brown eyes, cow and human, as if the Jersey wondered what she had done wrong, and Millie had a soft heart for disobedient cows. He pointed the critter toward the quartermaster stables.

"Not to the hospital?" Millie asked.

Ted felt only relief that she seemed willing to overlook his brisk handling of the Jersey. "Not the hospital. I think the major wants to make an example of these felons and miscreants," Ted told her. He winced inwardly to think how silly he sounded, but Millie only dimpled up as though he truly was a witty man.

What do I say now? What now? he asked himself with some desperation as Millie ambled along with him to the quartermaster stables, blessedly some distance away. "Um, uh, how do you like working at the hospital?" he asked, at a loss.

"Well enough," she replied, skipping to keep up with him. He slowed down. "I like to cook, and we do have better ingredients to work with."

"What would you make with the milk?" he asked, curious now.

"Butter, and perhaps cottage cheese. Probably a creamed stew involving canned oysters," she replied, with no hesitation. "Creamed chipped beef on toast points."

Ted started to salivate. He wiped his mouth and hoped she didn't notice.

She did; he watched her dimple play about in her cheek after she glanced his way. "Perhaps you had better come down with an epic disease and find out," she teased, which made him want to wriggle like a puppy.

"Nope. Strong as an ox," he said. He couldn't remember the last time he had been sick. Obviously hard tack and sowbelly on the march agreed with him. His palate must be immune to the tender ministrations of constantly revolving enlisted men in E Company who took their turn cooking, no matter what their culinary skills.

Bless Millie Drummond's heart, but she seemed to understand he was just one more corporal, healthy or not, rendered tongue-tied by her presence. As they herded three cows from the parade ground to the stable, she told him about the various garrisons she had lived in, and her last two years spent in Minnesota attending school and living with a beloved aunt.

"She said I could easily find a husband among all the lumberjacks," Millie said, "but I missed the West. She gave me her blessing to leave."

Ted silently uttered his own prayer of gratitude to a woman he had never met, who hadn't held Millie hostage. The men of Minnesota could snoop about among their own to find brides. Out here in Dakota Territory, the pool of bridal material was so miniscule as to be nonexistent.

The cows were duly turned into the corral behind the quartermaster storehouse to serve out their sentence. Ted looked down at the memo in his gloved hands, wondering what storm was about to break over Captain Crampton's head. Ted knew him as a surgeon who never minded making house calls to either Officers Row or Suds Row. Hopefully he would take the memo in good grace and end the matter.

He wanted Millie to talk with him back to the hospital, and he waited as she stood a long moment, arms on the corral fence, just watching the hospital cows. When she turned, her expression was thoughtful.

Taking a cue from Millie, he told her about his own route to Dakota Territory, admitting he hadn't enjoyed farming or cows much. Soldiering suited him well enough and he said as much to the pretty miss walking by his side, now that he was smart enough to shorten his stride to accommodate her.

"Papa likes soldiering too," she told him.

Might as well ask. "Do you mind moving from place to place?" he asked. A man ought to know that much, if he planned any sort of campaign involving a sergeant's daughter.

"I don't mind," she said, after favoring him with a shy glance. "It might be fun to settle down sometime, but so far I haven't found a spot I minded leaving."

He felt more or less the same way, but he couldn't think of another question, not with the hospital right in front of them. Duty called and he could not ignore it, as much as he wished to. He held up the memo.

"This might be an ugly scene," he said. "Thanks for keeping me company, Miss Drummond," he said.

"It's Millie," she said quietly. She touched his arm with light fingers, then hurried toward the back of the hospital from whence kitchen fragrances originated. He went down the hall and knocked on Captain Crampton's door.

"Come in," he heard and opened the door. He saluted, and handed the memo to the surgeon, who read it and frowned. The post surgeon stuck his head out the door and called, "Corporal Roach!"

In a moment, the hospital steward appeared, wiping his hands on an apron with questionable yellow stains.

Captain Crampton showed him the memo. The hospital steward frowned too. "I am certain they were grazing behind the hospital, last time I looked," he said.

Captain Crampton tapped the memo. "Obviously not now." He looked at Ted. "Major Brotherton is really going to fine me three dollars for this silliness?"

"I believe he is, sir," Ted replied, wishing he had a better answer. "One dollar per cow."

"My steward here says they were grazing behind the hospital," the post surgeon said, obviously not a man to yield gracefully.

"They may have been at one time, sir," Ted told him, "but I found, um, evidence on the parade ground, and they were definitely between the houses on Officers Row when I apprehended them."

The post surgeon rummaged in his desk and pulled out a prescription pad. "Give this to Major Brotherton," he said, ripping off his own memo.

Ted took it and stared down at handwriting so illegible that he turned it sideways for a better look. Captain Crampton snatched it back and tried again. He gave the second memo to Ted. "It says I will be down to see him later on, after

I debride a burn, stitch a laceration, and recast a leg."

Ted knew better than to turn this memo sideways, even though it looked no more readable than the first. He saluted and left the hospital, resisting the urge to smile until he was well down the boardwalk path.

He watched Major Brotherton turn the memo sideways before telling the man just what the post surgeon had written. Another smart salute, and Ted beat a dignified retreat. He left orders with the sergeant of the guardhouse to send a detail with bucket and shovels to do justice to the parade ground, then returned to his temporary domain in the officer of the guard building.

Ted made his own entries in the day's record book, wondering if Millie Drummond would be interested in civilian life. During a glorious afternoon of free time recently in Bismarck after picking up the upriver mail at Fort Lincoln, he had wandered to Gilhooly's Photography. He had spent several hours watching the man work, and even assisted in the darkroom. The Irishman assured Ted he had a knack for developing and told him to stop by when he was next downriver, and try the actual camera.

"I could use a dependable assistant with a sure eye and temperate ways," Martin Gilhooly told him when they shook hands and parted. "Too many drunks in Bismarck."

"I never really thought about a career besides the army," he had said to Mr. Gilhooly.

"Maybe you should, boyo," had been the Irishman's reply.

That "maybe you should" followed him around for the rest of the afternoon in Bismarck. Floating a few feet off the ground, Ted Sheppard had even stopped at Larsen's Jewelry and Fine Goods and looked at wedding rings, the delicate kind that would appear to good advantage on the finger of a lass with red hair. He found just the ring, because he had that sure eye, but those temperate ways kept him from buying it.

He closed the record book and wondered if Millie Drummond preferred the moveable life of a sergeant's wife to something more settled in a place like say, Bismarck, married to a civilian with ambitions to open his own photographic studio someday. Ted knew he would make sergeant if he re-upped in two years for another five-year enlistment, but the idea of a future other than the army intrigued him. Would it intrigue Millie Drummond? And how would he really know if she cared for him? A man couldn't just ask, after all, or could he?

So he stewed and fretted, and did his duty when called upon that afternoon. Not until shadows were lengthening across the buildings did the matter of the hospital cows come to Corporal Sheppard's attention again.

He was filling in at the guardhouse next door while the sergeant of the guard hurried to some unnamed crisis in K Troop's barrack. The prisoners sent to clean up the parade ground after the hospital cows' indiscretions had returned to their cells. At ease, Corporal Sheppard stood in the doorway, watching another messenger from the general vicinity of Major Brotherton's quarters head his way, his stride purposeful and no smile on his face this time.

After a salute, Ted opened the latest memo, where the words, "Report to me at once!" fairly leaped off the pale blue paper.

"The hospital?" Ted asked the orderly, who nodded, and finally permitted himself a smile.

"What a bumble broth this has become," the orderly said. "Less than an hour ago, the hospital steward showed up here with three dollars. Major Brotherton had me release the cows from debtors prison—"

"Which should have ended everything," Ted finished, ever hopeful.

"Only beginning! Captain Crampton had sent along his assistant steward to milk the ex-convicts right there." He gave an empty-handed gesture. "Only one quart for the three of them."

"Someone else milked the cows," Ted filled in.

"Captain Crampton is practically jumping up and down on his desk. He fired off a memo to the CO, and here I am," the orderly said. "The major wants you on the double, and I am to stay here and fill your position until you return."

Ted didn't feel the matter demanded a dead run, but he did hurry the long distance to the field officer's quarters. He was met at the door by Major Brotherton, looking as cold-eyed as Ted had ever seen the man.

The major nearly threw the dispatch at the corporal of the guard. "Take this to that . . . that quack who calls himself a surgeon!" Brotherton fairly shouted. "You are excused from retreat ceremony!"

"Sir?" Ted asked, startled at this hiccup in the day's order of business.

"I am ordering you to go from company mess hall to company mess hall. Check every pot and see if you can figure out who milked the surgeon's cows." The major gestured to the dispatch in Ted's hand. "I've told Captain Crampton to prefer a charge of falsehood against his steward and send the man to the guardhouse. On your way, Corporal."

The headache began before Ted covered half the distance to the hospital. It grew quickly worse when the post surgeon read the latest memo, cursed and swore and summoned his steward, a circumspect fellow and a bit of a priss.

As Corporal Sheppard tried to make himself small in the corner of the surgeon's office, Captain Crampton demanded to know exactly when the steward had seen the cows behind the hospital and not on the parade ground, as Major Brotherton claimed and all signs pointed.

Corporal Roach stammered, hemmed and hawed, and admitted he might have been wrong about his assertion.

"I'd prefer not to satisfy the major by charging you with anything, Roach," the post surgeon said finally, his voice more calm. "Might you have been mistaken about the time you claim to have seen the cows behind the hospital?"

"Quite likely, sir," Roach replied, not a man to press a highly charged issue, whatever the truth. "I must have been wrong."

"Dismissed," Captain Crampton said. "Go . . . go empty a bed pan."

Roach left with a salute and showed a clean pair of heels in his rapid retreat. The post surgeon scribbled another dispatch, looked at it, and printed a return message. "If he can't read my writing, tell the man my steward was mistaken," he said, leaning heavily on the desk and looking much older than he had looked only this morning. "I still want to know who milked those cows and where the milk is."

"Major Brotherton has ordered me to check every company mess kitchen and see what I can learn, sir," Ted assured him. "I'll find your culprit."

Captain Crampton gave him a wan smile and sent him packing too. After a swift return to a seething commanding officer, and an even quicker report to the sergeant of the guard, who had returned to the guardhouse, Ted Sheppard began his search for the criminal who had milked three hospital cows. He also wondered when the army had gone from a fearsome arm of the government's will to a carnival sideshow, at least at Fort Buford.

Word has a way of silently circulating around a typical garrison. Ted was met at each mess hall by a smiling company sergeant and the weekly cook, who showed him every pot and let him peer into every pan and cookstove oven. Fort Buford was a six-company post. By the time he completed his search and each company had finished supper—and who knows, eaten or drunk the evidence—Ted Sheppard found himself back at Major Brotherton's door after Retreat, unable to claim success.

If he had been bamboozled by an entire company, one of whose inmates had scavenged hospital milk from hospital cows, the bamboozlers won that day. Ted found nothing suspicious anywhere, beyond K Troop's larger-than-normal pile of raisins, which suggested someone had dipped into the commissary supplies unannounced. As he had not been sent to confiscate raisins, Ted overlooked it.

"I have nothing to report, sir," he told the major who was pouring himself something amber out of a crystal decanter.

Ted straightened his shoulders, ready to take the blistering scold he expected, deserved or not. To his surprise, Major Brotherton poured another drink and handed it to him without a word. Ted drank, saluted smartly, and left.

Ted's officer of the guard duties ended the next morning at Guard Mount when another lieutenant, sergeant, and corporal received their sashes for the twenty-four hour period and took over the guardroom at the edge of Fort Buford, ready to do the will of their commanding officer. He returned to his usual duties in E Company, drilling new recruits and supervising fatigue details.

Those naughty cows remained behind the hospital, more carefully watched by the assistant steward now. Ted thought briefly about accidentally running a bayonet through his arm, just for an excuse to go to the hospital and see

Millie, but dismissed that notion with the laugh it deserved. Maybe he would get up enough courage—he who had held off a whole cluster of irate Apaches when the Seventh Infantry served in the Southwest—to just knock on Sergeant Drummond's door and ask if he could sit with the man's lovely daughter.

Two days after the cow incident, Millie Drummond solved his problem.

After Recall from Fatigue, Millie joined him as he walked alone from the commissary storehouse to his barrack. One moment he walked by himself, and the next moment she walked beside him. He shortened his stride immediately, which brought at little pink to her cheeks, at least as much pink as showed in a lass with some Ojibwe ancestors.

"I didn't hear you," he said, which made her laugh and remind him that she had quiet ancestors on one side of her family tree.

She cleared her throat. "Mama said I could invite you to supper tonight," she said, looking straight ahead.

Dear heart, you are as shy as I am, but so much braver, he thought. "I would like that, Miss Drummond."

"Remember, it's Millie," she said, and turned back toward Suds Row. "See you at six, Corporal Sheppard."

"And I am Ted," he said softly to the empty air.

Ever punctual, Corporal Theodore Sheppard knocked on the Drummonds' door at precisely six of the clock, his lid tucked under his arm. Millie opened the door with a smile and ushered him in.

Sergeant Drummond had always intimidated Ted with his remarkable posture and his steely-eyed stare that suffered not a single fool gladly. This Sergeant Drummond in a checkered shirt, wool pants, and moccasins looked like a fellow who might enjoy a game of checkers or an evening's conversation. Ted felt himself relax.

Millie's smiling mother ushered them right to the table in the corner of the front room. He remembered in time to pull out Millie's chair for her, then seated himself beside her. It was a tight fit because the table was small, but he enjoyed every moment, breathing in the lavender fragrance in Millie's hair.

Sergeant Drummond asked a spartan Presbyterian blessing, then took the lid off the soup tureen. He ladled soup into a big bowl and handed it to Millie, who passed it to Ted, who stared down in shocked disbelief.

It was cream of oyster soup, milky and thick. The sutler sold canned oysters, and Ted knew how costly those tins were, because he had eyed them a time or two. But the cream?

"Some bread, Corporal?" Millie asked, as she handed him a plate with slabs of white bread baked by some angel from a celestial realm far from Dakota Territory. "Butter?"

He took the bread and stared at the butter, which bore no resemblance to the rancid stuff found in tins in the commissary storehouse. This was freshly made butter, the kind from contented, pampered cows who had just cost Captain Crampton three dollars. In mystified silence, he sliced off a hunk and buttered his bread.

In further silence, he filled his spoon with glorious soup and downed it, marveling at the exquisite mingling of cream with milk that had never been condensed and stuffed in a can to languish for years. He closed his eyes with the wonder of it, even as he had an entire series of questions that needed asking.

The sergeant cleared his throat and Ted put down his spoon.

"Millie, what do you have to say?" her father asked his lovely daughter, but in a tone most fatherly, and if Ted was listening right, singularly proud.

Millie looked at Ted, gazed deep into his eyes, and said so softly he had to lean closer to her, no hardship. "I'm the guilty party."

Those same eyes filled with tears, and one slid down beside her nose. Without even thinking, Ted took his napkin and dabbed at it gently.

"Tell him why, dear," Mrs. Drummond said.

"Corporal Petty's wife has a baby that just isn't thriving," she said in a whisper. "I thought maybe if she had some fortified milk, it would help. All I could think of was that wee one. I waited until the soldiers left after Recall from Fatigue and milked all three cows."

"No one saw you?" Ted asked.

She shook her head. "I can be so quiet. I took the milk to Mrs. Petty, and more milk to some of the children here on Suds Row. It was such a hard winter for children, and several still need feeding up. Have you ever noticed the Indian women who hang around the slaughterhouse, hoping for scraps? They don't actually beg, but their eyes follow you . . ." Her voice trailed away.

Ted nodded. He had seen them too, and felt hot shame that proud people had come to that, thanks to the government whose will he enforced.

"I thought they could use some too."

She was crying in earnest now. Ted didn't hesitate to put his arm around her. She turned her face into his side and he felt her shake. He handed her his handkerchief this time and she blew her nose.

"I brought the rest back here because I . . . I . . . Corporal, I wanted to fix you something good for supper," she finished in a rush. "Your face looks thin."

"It always has," he said, thinking of meals skipped and rough half-rations on campaign, and even poorer meals years earlier on a hardscrabble farm. The fact that she had been observing him touched Ted in a place so deep he knew he could never find it, even with a compass. "That's not new."

"Maybe not," she told him, and he heard firmness in her voice now, a resolve that told him he might someday be in capable hands, if he played his cards right with this kind woman. "I was too impulsive, Corporal, and I should apologize for what I did." She sat up, but didn't move too far from his orbit, to his relief. "Since you were corporal of the guard, I felt I owed you the explanation. Should I pay three dollars to the post surgeon? I could slip it on his desk and he would never know."

"I think he can stand the strain, Millie," Ted replied, trying out her name and finding it much to his liking. "Let's just call the whole matter a mystery."

Sergeant Drummond nodded. "She won't do it again, corporal."

"I wish she could," he said frankly. "What say you that I talk to the post surgeon and ask if there is anything we can do for those Indian women who beg for scraps? I helped inventory the commissary warehouse today and we have an amazing amount of rations." He chuckled. "And barrels of surplus raisins."

"Could you do that?" she asked, eager now, tears forgotten.

"If you call me Ted," he said, then amended it. "Or even if you don't. I may not succeed, but I can try."

He looked into her eyes again, those deep brown pools of kindness and compassion and concern for others, and decided right then to be a better man than he had been only minutes ago, when he was just a pretty good fellow. He thought if he spent more time around Millie Drummond, he would become better still. He knew he loved her.

"Your wonderful soup is getting cold, corporal," Sergeant Drummond said.

Ted gave Millie a slow wink and turned back to his cream of oyster soup, with its buttery sheen and little oyster crackers bobbing about as he stirred. He savored every mouthful, and then ate his bread and butter with relish. Her own dark eyes smiling, Mrs. Drummond brought out vanilla cream pudding, which made Corporal Sheppard laugh out loud.

When everything was devoured and Mrs. Drummond busied herself in the kitchen, Ted reached down into his growing vault of courage and asked Sergeant Drummond if he could sit for a while in the front room with his daughter.

"You may, corporal," replied the sergeant he had once feared. "I'm headed back to my barrack to check on my boys. I trust you'll dismiss yourself when the bugler sounds Tattoo." He smiled. "But come back anytime, eh, Millie?"

His stomach full, his heart more full, Ted Sheppard sat on the family sofa, made from a packing crate, and cuddled Millie Drummond. He had a million things to say to her, but they could all wait. He held her close and inclined his head toward hers. Maybe in a few more visits he could ask her opinion of Bismarck and photography, or her views on women's rights, or if she preferred dogs to cats, or any of those stupid little things that matter only to lovers.

It was enough now to hold her. He gave a discreet belch from all that rich food, and Millie laughed, but softly, so as not to alert her mother in the kitchen.

"I made butter cookies too," she whispered in his ear.

Mary Murphy

I met Mary Murphy on a train heading west to Fort Laramie. But I can't really say that I met her, because no one introduced us then, and no one ever did later, either.

I was just out of the academy. It was August, and after graduation in June, I had rushed through a furlough at Newport Beach with my folks, and then received my orders to Company K, Second Cavalry, garrisoned at Fort Laramie, Wyoming Territory. According to my orders, I was to stop at Omaha Barracks long enough to attach myself to ten new recruits for Company K and escort them West.

I remember even now the feeling I had as I stood in the middle of the parade ground at

Omaha Barracks and watched the heat shimmer off the quarters on Officers Row. I wondered what I was supposed to do. I had been assigned to the cavalry arm of the US Army, and Omaha Barracks was my first look at a cavalry post.

I eventually found my ten recruits. Some of them had served in the recent War of the Rebellion and reenlisted after busting out in civilian life. The others spoke German or Irish-accented English that I could barely understand. Most of them were older than I was. Luckily for all of us, a Sergeant O'Brien from Fort Laramie showed up before we departed. He piloted us West.

Mary's name was on the company roster the sergeant handed me before we pulled out— "Mary Murphy, twenty, white, single, laundress." The army hired females as laundresses to wash the company clothes. Each company of fifty to eighty men employed two or three laundresses, who received rations like the men and were paid one dollar per month by each soldier for doing his laundry. By 1877, most of the laundresses were replaced by wives of the soldiers, but this was 1875, and Mary was our laundress.

I noticed her when she got on the train, clutching a knotted bundle of clothing, a baby crooked in one arm, and a toddler dragging behind her. She was sweating like the rest of us, with half-moons of perspiration under her arms and a streak of sweat soaking through the back of her shirtwaist. That surprised me. I never really thought about women sweating. My mother never did nor any of the women I had even known.

The baby in her arms wasn't more than a few months old. It had her dark hair and a placid expression that seemed out of place on the hot, crowded train. The toddler had the bored look of a child who has been on the move constantly. He ran ahead of his mother, found an empty seat, and crawled up on it. He smiled when the soldier across the aisle handed him a sugar candy.

Mary came down the aisle, swaying a little to keep her balance as the train started to move. She saw me, paused, and smiled. It wasn't the usual ingratiating smile of an inferior but a relieved, patient kind of smile, as if I could help her.

The train lurched down the track, gathering speed, and the sudden motion threw Mary against the back of the seat in front of me. She stumbled and dropped her bundle but hung onto the baby, who started to cry. The soldier behind her put a hand on her waist for balance, and she blushed as the other men in the car nudged each other and snickered.

She sat down next to her boy, across the aisle from me. To quiet the baby, she opened her shirtwaist and began to nurse. I had never seen anything like that before. Mother had wet nurses for all of us, and the door to the nursery was always closed during feedings. Mary covered herself as best she could with her shirtwaist, and most of us looked away—including me.

The men who didn't turn their heads divided their time between staring at Mary, making low comments to their bunkies, and laughing at me. I knew that my face was red. I could feel it.

Mary's children were quiet most of that long, hot trip. The older boy (his name was Flynn) whimpered a bit in the heat as we chugged across Nebraska. I have never enjoyed crossing Nebraska, either by train or on horseback. It is either hot and flat or cold and flat. Anyway, Flynn was passed from soldier to soldier, and by the time we reached Cheyenne Depot, he had accumulated two revolvers carved out of soap, a wooden horse, and some jelly beans which melted and got all over my new boots.

It did take time to reach Cheyenne Depot. We were delayed by buffalo on the tracks and more often by hotboxes, when the axle-bearing joints heated up. The train had to stop and cool down before proceeding.

Mary's baby began to fret as we neared Cheyenne. Adele has told me since that Mary's milk was probably drying up, and the baby wasn't getting enough, but I didn't know anything then. Mary spent most of her time walking up and down the aisle, rocking the baby (I never did learn its name), and making crooning sounds. The baby developed a thin cry, and I noticed that whenever it started to wail, some of the older soldiers would look at each other. Sergeant O'Brien crossed himself a couple of times.

At Cheyenne Depot, the horses were unloaded, and there was a Dougherty wagon from the fort to meet us. It filled up quickly. There were two captains' wives and children from first class to fit in, plus some of their luggage. There wasn't any room for Mary and her children in the wagon, so the tailgate was lowered, and they perched on that.

The other women stayed as far away from Mary as they could, and I heard one of the wives commanding her children not to play with Flynn. I'm sure Mary heard too, but her face was peaceful. She hugged her crying baby and sang to it.

The baby cried more and more, with a gasping sound that made me wish the surgeon was along. I found myself riding back by the Dougherty to check on the baby. They were eating dust back there. Flynn choked and sputtered until a private swung him up in his saddle and rode back toward the front of the column.

We camped that night at Lodgepole Creek, and Mary's baby kept me awake. Not because it was crying, because by then, it wasn't crying. It struggled and fought for breath in the heat that refused to leave us, even after the sun went down.

I found myself breathing along with the baby. I heard Mary whispering Hail Mary over and over, and my lips moved along with hers in the dark on the other side of the Dougherty.

I will never forget the second night out when we halted just before dusk at Chug Station. Mary jumped off the wagon before it rolled to a complete stop and hurried to the sergeant. She gestured to the baby, and I couldn't hear what she said, but O'Brien dismounted as if his saddle were on fire and bent over the infant. He called to me.

"Lieutenant, this baby's dead."

Heads poked out of the Dougherty wagon and then were pulled in again.

The baby was dead. It was even getting a little stiff.

"How long, Mary?" the sergeant asked.

"Since before the last rest stop." Mary's voice quavered, and she looked at me. "I just couldn't say anything."

That was the first time I had ever seen anyone dead before. That dead baby touched me more than I care to remember, and I have seen much death here on the plains in the twenty years since. The baby's eyes were closed, and the dark hair was curly and damp from Mary's perspiration. Except for a china-doll appearance that made my knees weak, the baby looked asleep.

The sergeant detailed a couple of privates to dig a little grave under a cottonwood by the river. Mary wrapped her shawl around the body and handed it to me.

"Here, please," she begged. "I can't do it."

I knelt by the hole and put the baby in. Mary covered her face with her hands, and I saw tears running through her fingers. The other women stayed near the wagon. I knew why. They had been taught, same as I, to avoid women like Mary, those bits of flotsam without husbands and with a string of children who followed the army from post to post. Mary needed comfort, but none of us gave her any.

Mary clung to Flynn the rest of the journey, her face wearing a white, transfigured look that I could see even under the road dust that covered all of us. She clutched her little boy to her and hung onto the chains that held the tailgate.

The remainder of the trip is still a painful memory. I was the ranking officer. With the death of that baby, responsibility for the lives of others descended on me and has been a burden ever since. And when Mary looked at me with her patient expression, I knew I was ill equipped.

Once we arrived at Fort Laramie, I forgot about Mary. Well, I did think about her every time my laundry was returned washed, ironed, and folded neatly on top of my campaign trunk. She did a good job with shirts. There were none of the little scorch marks and wrinkles I later came to associate with army life. I almost slipped a note in with my dirty clothes one day to let her know that I appreciated the good job, but I reconsidered. I didn't even know if she could read.

I didn't think much about Mary until a year later. In the early spring of 1876, Mary came to my attention again.

I was officer of the guard. It was around eleven o'clock at night, and I had just stretched out on the officer-of-the-day's cot. I hated sleeping in the guardhouse. It was infested with graybacks, and just the thought of that made me start to itch. Down below me that night in the cells were a private sleeping off a mighty drunk and a German corporal waiting for garrison court-martial.

It was the night after payday. The army was paid every two months then, and that usually meant pretty intense card playing and drinking until the money was in someone else's pockets.

The sergeant of the guard came puffing up from Suds Row and hollered to me to come quick. A corporal in the band had been drinking and had knifed his wife.

By the time I got there, she was already dead. He had slit her throat from ear to ear, and there was a mild, surprised look in her wide-open eyes that made me turn away. Blood was everywhere—on the ceiling, on the walls, and splattered on the iron stove, where it bubbled and stank.

The corporal was drunk and just beginning to realize what he had done. The sergeant jerked his hands behind his back and bound them tight with a rawhide thong. The two of them lurched across the slippery floor, heading for the guardhouse.

I heard children crying in the kitchen. I went in there to look and to get away from the awful mess in the front room.

Mary Murphy sat there with the children. She was holding two blood-daubed little girls on her lap. She was in her nightgown, which was flecked with blood. Again, she gave me that patient, relieved smile, and, again, I didn't know what to do for her.

"Can you take the children?" I asked her finally, "At least, for a while?"

"Yes, certainly, Lieutenant." Her voice had the Irish lilt so common back then in the Indian-fighting army.

While I supervised the removal of the body from the front room, Mary must have left with the children. When I looked in the kitchen later, they were gone.

The next morning, sometime before First Call, the corporal worked his hands free and looped his belt with his neck in it over the bolt in the wall of his solitary cell. He wasn't in my company, but as I filled out the report, the adjutant assigned me to track down any living relatives to find a home for the orphans. As was the case in too many of these situations, I couldn't find anyone.

Mary kept the girls. I know now what a burden that must have been to her, because when Adele and I had children, we had trouble making ends meet on officer's pay. Mary was doing it on a laundress's wages.

A few weeks after the incident, our company was sent north in time to get all the stuffing beat out of us by Crazy Horse on the Rosebud. I took an arrow in the back and was invalided back to Fort Laramie. While I was recovering,

I did a lot of walking and often went down to the river. Mary was always there with the other laundresses, dipping water in good and bad weather, and washing down there on the bank when it was hot. She scrubbed, pounded, and beat the clothes on her washboard, all the time singing and talking to Flynn and the two little girls who clung to her skirts. They played at the river's edge and made mud pies on the ground near her washtub. A month later, I was promoted and transferred to Company B, Second Cavalry (I knew someone influential in DC), then posted to Fort Bowie, Arizona Territory.

I never saw Mary again. I met Adele in Massachusetts a few years later while on furlough, and we have spent much of our time here in the Southwest. Whenever Adele and I quarrel, which isn't too often, I think of Mary and her patient smile and wonder whatever became of her. I imagine she raised those children by herself. They are probably married now, with children of their own.

Well, never mind. Mary Murphy. I think of her.

A Leader of His Troops

First Sergeant Hiram Chandler, C Company, Third Cavalry, knew better than to laugh at a superior officer, but he was hard put not to turn away and blame his chortles on a coughing fit every time Lieutenant Arthur Shaw, currently commanding C Company, popped into the adjutant's office to check for mail. It was at least the second time since that morning's Guard Mount, so Hiram had to wonder just how a letter was supposed to materialize, since nothing had arrived by courier yet.

Hiram had a bird's eye view to watch his lieutenant, seated as he was on his remount and dragging some new recruits through a bit of equitation on the parade ground. The winter had been typically long and dreary at Fort Fetterman, located on a bend in the Platte River. One result was penned-up, snuffy horses needing exercise and seeming to feel no regret at tossing troopers.

His own, well-mannered gelding gave a shake to the reins, as if dismayed at the horses and riders and wondering how on earth these soldiers would survive an upcoming season of endless patrol.

"They'll figure it out," Hiram said out loud to his horse, but not loud enough for the troopers to hear. "Amazing how an Indian war whoop sharpens the intellect."

As for his lieutenant, Hiram admitted to feeling some of the man's pain. This morning, Lieutenant Shaw had given Hiram a bleak look that said "No letters." When they walked together to company barracks to make fatigue assignments, Shaw had heaved a mighty sigh.

"I as much as proposed in that last letter, sergeant, and did Miss Hinchcliffe bother to reply? Not on your tintype. What is wrong with women? It's 1878! These are modern times!"

Maybe she's saying no by her non reply, you dolt, Hiram thought. "Give her time, sir. Marriage is a big decision," was the best he could offer. He had his own concerns.

Thinking about those concerns made him choose mercy over justice and release the troopers with enough time to feed and groom their horses and answer the bugler blowing Mess Call. Hiram ate his beans and bread with grape jelly with C Company's other sergeant, who looked scarcely more cheerful than their lieutenant.

They knew each other pretty well. A raised eyebrow in Sergeant Crosby's direction had given the man permission to unload about his own troubles with the US Mail and why in the Sam Hill nothing ever seemed to come his way from Connecticut.

Hiram listened, something he did well. His impromptu training had begun early in his army career, after the Battle of Cold Harbor. Hardly anyone else in his company survived and his commanding officer, a grim-lipped lieutenant, had needed a sergeant, any sergeant, in the worst way. The job was Hiram's, for good or ill. Since he was only sixteen and greener than grass, he learned to listen. The less he said the wiser he looked, and truth to tell, if the man with the grievance talked long enough, he could usually solve his own problem.

The technique did not fail him even now, when he really wanted to spill out his own problems, instead of listen to someone else's. Almost against his will he listened, and sure enough, Sergeant Crosby solved his own problem.

"Ah, well, Hiram, my sweetheart and I have weathered other assaults by the US Mail," he said, after chasing the last bean around his tin plate. "This is my last five-year enlistment."

"Then it's back to Connecticut and a wedding?" Hiram asked, even though he knew the answer. It had been the subject of many a sergeants' gathering.

"High time!" Sergeant Crosby gave up on the bean and stood up, ready for work and cheerful now, because Sergeant Chandler had listened. "You ever going to do something similar?" he asked Hiram, but didn't wait for an answer. He left the mess hall whistling.

"I'm in love with Birdie O'Grady," Hiram said softly to the retreating back. "I'm waiting for a letter too."

Mary Bertha O'Grady, to be proper. He had met her at distant Fort Laramie at the same time Lieutenant Shaw had met Miss Virginia Hinchcliffe because Birdie was Miss Hinchcliffe's maid. Birdie had been struggling with her mistress's luggage at the Rustic Hotel, where the Cheyenne-Deadwood stage had dropped them off last year, and C Company had chanced to be escorting the mail from Fetterman.

Lieutenant Shaw had been a no-hoper from the first, when Miss Hinchcliffe batted her pretty blues at him and asked for help to Major Dunlap's quarters. "Mrs. Major Dunlap is my sister," she said, "and I've come to help out."

"Help out" was generally a euphemism for providing nursemaid services for a new baby, and giving the Eastern damsel a chance to look over prospects in the unmarried officer corps. In Miss Hinchcliffe's case, Birdie O'Grady had been saddled with nursemaid duties, while the ladies played and Miss Hinchcliffe flirted.

She had been selective in her flirting, not wasting a moment's time with officers who had no useful Eastern connections. The Shaw name and the Boston locale had caused her to target Lieutenant Shaw whenever he appeared at Fort Laramie from Fort Fetterman. Somehow that summer he appeared a lot, which meant Hiram invariably came along too.

Having caught the eye of the most congenial Birdie O'Grady, Hiram began to press his own advantage. It had been a simple matter to drop in on the pretty maid when he saw her on the Dunlap porch, pushing a cradle on its rockers. By the time autumn arrived, which meant sudden cold and snow far too early, he knew she was from County Kerry, twenty-two, and fortunate to have caught the Hinchliffes' eye when they toured Ireland five years ago.

"No future in Ireland, so I went to Philadelphia with the Hinchliffes," she said.

An observant listener, he saw and heard her little sigh. "Do you miss County Kerry?" Hiram had asked.

She nodded and said nothing, but turned her attention to the baby. He kept watching her face, and saw her dab at her eye when she probably thought he was paying more attention to something on the parade ground.

After a moment of fussing with the little one, she turned her attention to him, her expression most kindly. Gadfreys, but she was a pretty girl, with deep red hair and brown eyes.

"Did you cry the first time you left home?" she had asked straight out, no varnish.

He had not, and he knew the truth was in order, because he did not want to lie to this charming woman. He told her about waiting to get up the nerve to leave the tyranny of his father's farm, where so much labor fell to him because his older brothers had joined the Union Army. He didn't say too much about that tyranny; even now it was a sore spot.

"Did you ever go back home, Sergeant?" she asked.

"Once," he admitted, and continued his truth telling. "We were all uncomfortable and I was soon on my way to Fort Hays in Nebraska." He shrugged. "I write now and then."

She had given him a sympathetic eye, as if wondering about families who did not love and cherish each other. "I cried a lot of nights," she told him, "and then I realized that was pointless. I am here, and here I'll stay. Honestly, I like America."

Hiram found his way to the major's porch two or three more times before C Company, led by an even more reluctant Lieutenant Shaw, dragged itself away from Fort Laramie and returned to an isolated and suddenly more dreary Fort Fetterman.

Once he got over the mopes on that return journey, Lieutenant Shaw went into mile after mile of rapture over Miss Hinchcliffe. Since Captain Harvey, titular head of C Company, wasn't the man for a lieutenant's small talk, and the company's second lieutenant was on detached duty, Sergeant Chandler ended up listening, whether he wanted to or not.

"She is of the Philadelphia Hinchcliffes," the man had crowed, which only made Sergeant Chandler, raised on a poor and pathetic farm, wonder just how many breeds of Hinchcliffe inhabited the thirty-eight states. "We're going back to Fort Laramie in December for the Christmas party," the lieutenant had declared. "I don't care how deep the snow is."

Privately, Hiram didn't care, either. He wanted to see Birdie O'Grady. Publicly, he worried as the thermometer crowded down deep in the bowl. Eighty miles was nothing to C Company in the summer, but in the winter?

The journey had to be accomplished, and not only because Lieutenant Shaw was a self-absorbed, spoiled young officer. Their company captain finally received a long-sought, three-month furlough to see his family in Rhode Island. C Company's bold little band of volunteers was to escort Captain Harvey as far as Fort Laramie, where he could catch the Shy-Dead stage to Cheyenne and the Union Pacific.

"Only volunteers for the escort," Captain Harvey had stipulated firmly. "That's eighty nasty miles of frostbite I don't want on my conscience."

There were enough takers, knowing most Indians had more wisely hunkered down on reservations, where they would idle away a winter, then bolt in late spring to harass the US Army, as usual. Say what you want about the Lakota, they were nobody's fool.

Captain Harvey had surprised Hiram by taking him aside in his quarters the day before they were to leave. He even poured him a glass of better bourbon than the sutler's store sold and took Hiram into his confidence.

"When I'm home, I'll try for another three-month extension," the captain said, after clinking glasses. "That puts Lieutenant Shaw in command for six months. I'm certain I don't need to tell you that he bears watching."

"Yes, sir," Hiram said, aware of Shaw's many failures of command, most of which he had smoothed over because he was a long-time first sergeant and knew his business. "I am to keep him alive and teach him something without him knowing it."

Captain Harvey had the good grace to laugh. "That is why men like you are so valuable to the army." He leaned forward until the distance separating them had narrowed. "Sadly, Lieutenant Shaw is one of those pea-greeners who doesn't even know how little he knows. Do your best, Sergeant; the army is counting on you."

The captain laughed, maybe loosened up by the bourbon. "Shouldn't admit this, but every night I pray, 'Now I lay me down to sleep, I pray the Lord my soul to keep. If I die before my time, please make Artie Shaw resign.'"

A huge smile on his face, Hiram assured his commanding officer he would make every effort to keep C Company alive and well, and so the matter stood. The trip to Fort Laramie had been accomplished with no frostbite, and Captain Harvey was seen off on a well-deserved furlough. C Company was granted two glorious days to enjoy Fort Laramie and the annual enlisted men's ball, to which officers and ladies were invited.

The corporal and four privates who had volunteered had brought along their dress uniforms. Sergeant Chandler hadn't bothered. Wise in the ways of humanity, he had no doubt that Birdie O'Grady would be collared for baby-tending duty. A less self-assured man would have brought along his own dress uniform, with its admittedly impressive hashmarks denoting years of hard service. That man was not Hiram Chandler. If Birdie admitted him into Major Dunlap's quarters, he wasn't going to waste a minute on small talk, or be uncomfortable in a high collar.

For all he knew she had captured some Fort Laramie sergeant's eye and was married already; such things happened frequently at army posts. Not a wagering man, Hiram was still willing to bet that she had remained single. There had been something in her eyes when they said goodbye after their first meeting, a tenderness he had seen once before in another lady's eyes before war and then death had separated them.

With no patience at all, Hiram waited until eight o'clock, when the dinner and dance were underway, then walked to Major Dunlap's house.

His heart skipped a medically impossible beat when Birdie O'Grady opened the door, baby in her arms.

He knew he had never seen anyone lovelier. Her hair was untidy and stuck into a funny little bun. Her eyes looked full of tears, which caused him some alarm. Maybe she had been hoping someone else would tap on her door. But no, the dimple in her left cheek appeared, and her eyes grew a little smaller as her smile increased.

"Why in the world were you crying, Miss O'Grady?"

"Birdie to you," she said, and tucked the baby on her hip. Her gaze grew suddenly clear-eyed and he realized she was not a small talker, either. "I was afraid you had gone to the dance, like any sensible man who lives in an awful place like Fetterman, if I can believe rumors."

Heavens almighty, that voice! He could listen to her read the Manual of Arms and be entertained for hours. Her Irish lilt did more strange things to his heart. His was an Irish and a German army, this US Army after the war, and Hiram had heard many an accent. Not one of them had ever inclined him to want to kiss the speaker. He knew better, even now, but just barely.

She had asked him in, pointing him to the sofa and not an armchair, because she must have wanted to sit beside him. He sat and she lowered herself carefully next to him, her hand on the baby's head now, the child protected against any jostling. A little worm in Hiram's ear suggested she would be even more watchful of her own babies, and his face grew warm. He doubted he had blushed in twenty years, but here it came.

"I didn't think you would be at the dance, Birdie," he told her, and took a deeper breath. "I also wasn't sure you were still a single lady. I know the frontier army."

She laughed at that, a hearty sound that warmed him down to his toes. "Miss Hinchcliffe made me promise I would do no such thing."

That same little ear worm inclined him to speak up. "True, I suppose, but what punishment could she enact if you had accepted some . . . some . . ."

". . . sergeant's?"

"Yes, for the sake of argument, some sergeant's proposal? Fire you? You'd be married. So what?"

Again that laugh, but softer, because the baby seemed to be settling into her breast and neck. "Between you and me, Miss Hinchcliffe is not at her best whilst thinking."

He mulled that over, imagining what a fine match Miss Hinchcliffe would be for Lieutenant Shaw, who had graduated somewhere near the murky bottom of West Point Class of '75. But no, perhaps one of them should marry into brains. He shook his head and did his best not to snort.

"It is a bit frightening, Sergeant," she whispered, and turned slightly. "Is the baby asleep?"

"Yes. And call me Hiram."

She rose slowly and sort of glided out of the room, which kept the baby asleep, but also set her skirts to swaying in a manner so pleasing he had to look away to maintain any composure.

She soon returned to the parlor and sat beside him. He wasn't certain what to do until she looked at him with those beautiful brown eyes. His arm went around her shoulder. Since she didn't bat him away and cry foul, he continued breathing.

Without any encouragement, Hiram told her about his hard life on that Iowa farm, and his even harder eighteen months in the Union Army, beginning with the Battle of the Wilderness, and ending with the surrender at Appomattox. He handed her his handkerchief after the Battle of Spotsylvania Courthouse when he told her about stepping on top of still-writhing wounded men to continue firing into the Bloody Angle.

She handed it back for Cold Harbor as he blubbered and wiped his eyes. "Six times, Birdie. Why would any general make us charge six times?"

Her head rested on his shoulder through the Grand Army Review in Washington and then his Indian Wars years. He wanted to hear her life story next, and she began, but it ended quickly when they heard booted feet stamping off snow on the front porch. In a flash she was up and opening the door for the major and his wife, and then Miss Hinchcliffe with two lieutenants trailing behind her, one of them his own.

No one said anything about his presence in the parlor, but Hiram hoped what he noticed in Major Dunlap's one good eye was a little twinkle. Everyone said good night to everyone else and he found himself on that porch now. The door closed, then opened again and there stood Birdie O'Grady.

She gave him another serious look, the kind that meant business of a sort he had hoped for all his life, even if he did live in a dry-bone garrison in a territory full of testy Indians and earned thirty dollars a month.

She didn't say anything, but mouthed the words, "Please write to me," then closed the door.

And he had. Now he waited like Lieutenant Shaw, eager for a word from a lady, and wondering why in tarnation the US Mail had forgotten Fort Fetterman.

Two days later, Hiram knew it was not his place to say anything to his superior officer, but he wasn't surprised when Lieutenant Shaw moped around the guardhouse while Hiram released a C Company miscreant, and waited for the room to clear out.

"Sir?" Hiram asked, knowing that was enough to get his lieutenant to bare his soul, a somewhat shallow mechanism, as far as the sergeant could tell.

"Sergeant, did I mention to you that in my last letter to Miss Hinchcliffe, I hinted I would be asking her an important question?"

So you told me; the more fool you, Hiram thought, amused. He probably knew even less about courtship than his lieutenant, but Hiram did not think it wise to mention something so vital to a man's future happiness in a letter, or even to be so coy about it. "Brave of you, sir," he replied, because Shaw seemed to expect a comment.

"Brave? Brave? I wrote that letter eight weeks ago, and have I heard a single word from her since? D'ya think she has a clue what I meant? Has she rejected me?"

Hiram considered how to answer. Birdie O'Grady had remarked unfavorably on Miss Hinchcliffe's mental acuity, so that was one consideration. Maybe she truly was clueless. Or maybe she had rejected this lieutenant and didn't know how to put it in writing. An even more unhelpful scenario rose: perhaps Miss Hinchcliffe had already scarpered off to Ohio, dragging the dutiful Birdie along.

"We . . . I mean you . . . just won't know until a letter comes through, sir," he said finally.

192

Shaw swore long and fluently, which suggested too much time spent in the company of teamsters. Hiram could have done the same, because he was desperate to hear from Birdie, but he had better manners.

There the matter rested for nearly the entire month of May, with Lieutenant Shaw becoming increasingly sarcastic and morose in turns. Hiram was an expert at keeping his own counsel, but he longed to hear from Birdie. On a day with no wind and not much to do, he had walked to the non-commissioned officers' quarters and noted one empty duplex. He had looked in all the windows, putting imaginary furniture here and there.

He felt his own hopes begin to fade along with his lieutenant's, but he kept his misery to himself. News of the coming of the paymaster brought army business to the forefront over real or nonexistent affairs of the heart. The army was supposed to pay its soldiers every two months, but it had been six months since the ambulance carrying any paymaster of any kind had pulled up to the fort with his strong box full of heavily discounted greenbacks and a list of what was due every man, from Captain Coates, commanding, to the greenest private.

Hiram liked to be paid as well as the next soldier, but he was a provident fellow, and always hung onto enough salary to tide him over during financial drought. He loaned a little here and there if he knew the need was great, but never at moneylender rates. He preferred the good will of his men.

Amazing how a garrison could perk up at the dry announcement that the paymaster had arrived and would give every man what was due him directly after Guard Mount tomorrow. Years of experience assured Hiram what would follow, once the men had finished their day's duties. Those who owed the bloodsuckers would end up forking over a large amount of their pathetic salary to those who had loaned, with bitter words often exchanged, and occasional mayhem.

Even though excess was forbidden, someone always managed to get hold of beer and harder stuff, and the drinking commenced, accompanied by fierce gambling until the garrison was broke again. The guardhouse would be full of many sinners.

The barracks fairly buzzed with anticipation that night. Hiram shook his head at the noise and went to his own room, probably the best perquisite attached to his rank. He didn't have to share his space with bunkmates.

He was reading *Huckleberry Finn* on his bed, boots off, moccasins on, when the barracks grew quiet. The sergeant raised himself up on one elbow, suddenly alert.

Without even knocking, Lieutenant Shaw burst into his room, waving several letters that looked well-traveled, maybe even stomped on by buffalo. He slammed the door shut behind him and slumped into the room's only chair, his face a study in desperation. Hiram feared the worst from Miss Hinchcliffe.

"Sir?" he asked finally, when Shaw seemed unable to form words.

The lieutenant waved the letters again, but more feebly. "The paymaster handed these to me," he said finally. "He had got them from Fort Robinson, where they went astray, heaven knows when." He held them out dramatically. "Here are the two letters I sent to Miss Hinchcliffe. She hasn't heard from me in three months, Hiram, three months!"

"Well, uh . . ."

Shaw was far from done. He held out another letter, this one open, but bearing few signs of travel to and from Fort Rob. "Then this just arrived! Read it and weep."

Trying not to smile, Hiram took the letter from his lieutenant's shaking hand. "Are you certain, sir? I'd rather not read a lady's correspondence."

"Hang it all," Shaw snapped, grabbing back the letter. "I'll boil down the nasty thing. The love of my life, the future mother of my children, has assured me that if she doesn't hear from me or see me before June 4, she is taking the Shy-Dead to Cheyenne and walking out of my life forever."

As if on cue, both men's heads swiveled to look at Hiram's calendar, with each day neatly marked off down to May 30.

You are such a pup, Hiram thought, remembering their captain's admonition to keep Lieutenant Shaw out of trouble and learning his duties. "Sir, we'll be escorting the paymaster to Fort Laramie," Hiram reminded the lieutenant. "He'll pay the officers and men tomorrow. If we leave early the following day, I believe we'll make it to Fort Laramie on time. It takes three days, if we move along smartly. We'll get there at sundown on the third, and you'll have time to kneel at her feet and propose."

Shaw gave him a hard stare, then began to relax. "I believe you're right. There won't be time for spectacle. I had hoped to make an occasion of it, with champagne and perhaps the Fort Laramie glee club to serenade her."

"You probably still can, sir," Hiram said, at his soothing best. He had noticed another letter. "Sir, you have another letter."

"Yes, yes. It's for you. Here."

Shaw stood up. He opened up the door to Hiram's potbellied stove and tossed the unread letters into the flames. "I am going to speak to the paymaster, and do my dead-level best to convince him to quit this place with our escort as early as possible the day after tomorrow, or even tomorrow. Sergeant, have six men ready to ride on June 1 or sooner."

"Aye, sir," Hiram said with a salute which Shaw did not return, because he was already out the door and off on his mission to move the paymaster along.

Shaw lay down again, Huck Finn forgotten. He opened Birdie O'Grady's letter, wondering as he did so if she was the sort of woman to declare ultimatums like her mistress.

To his relief, but not his surprise, Birdie was not. There was no feminine vitriol on the closely written pages, no complaint because letters had not been forthcoming. It was only another kind letter, this one asking how he did, and telling him a little more about herself. He read it through twice, pleased that he would see her soon. He had roughly the same plan in mind as his lieutenant, but without champagne or singers. If she said yes, that empty duplex at Fetterman would be soon inhabited. Miss Hinchcliffe would fire her servant, but as he had pointed out to Birdie at Christmas, what did it matter? He slept soundly that night, with Birdie O'Grady's letter under his pillow.

Following Guard Mount the next morning, no one dispersed to the day's fatigue duties and drill. Anticipation writ large on many a face, the garrison with its two companies of infantry and one of cavalry, assembled in front of the adjutant's office, where the paymaster, a pale, glum-looking fellow name of Captain Perkins, had set up his table.

Since the men were paid in the order of their company commander's seniority, C Company came in dead last. As Sergeant Hiram Chandler stood at attention with his troops, Lieutenant Shaw sloped over to chat, not at his sparkling best.

"I tried to get that dratted man to leave right after he finishes here, but Captain Perkins is a milky boy with dyspepsia and vertigo," he whispered out of the corner of his mouth. "He says it has been a trying month of travel and he must rest today."

"We'll still make it, sir," Hiram said, in his soothing best. He wondered just how many more five-year enlistments he could tolerate before officers drove him crazy. Maybe Birdie O'Grady would have some wisdom about the future.

No trooper in C Company wasted a minute when it was his turn at the desk. Each man knew to sign the payroll, remove the white glove from his right hand, receive his handful of greenbacks, and salute with the left hand. Fetterman's company laundresses stood to one side, ready to receive their payment from each soldier, because it was the law that they be paid before any sprees.

Sergeant Chandler took a good look at Captain Perkins, gauging the paymaster's fitness and hoping the man wouldn't drag his feet and insist on another day at Fort Fetterman. He thought it unlikely, because no one wanted to spend one more day at that unfortunate post than he had to.

That evening, Hiram joined the other sergeants in keeping some sort of order in a post that hadn't been paid in half a year. He watched men stagger about from too much beer, oversaw a few card games, broke up several fights, and escorted members of the garrison to the guardhouse. He slept less soundly.

The morning brought overcast skies threatening snow, even this late in May, and a trembling Captain Perkins, who appeared scarcely better off than the men in the guardhouse sleeping away the remnants of payday.

"Sergeant, don't even give him a chance to cry sickness and spend another day here," Lieutenant Shaw said through tight lips.

Hiram soon learned that Captain Perkins had no intention of prolonging his stay at Fort Fetterman, but he did intend to complain and scold about such a desolate piece of US government property, as though anyone in C Company could make it better.

Help came from a surprising source. As the escort mounted and waited more or less patiently—less patient was Lieutenant Shaw—for Captain Perkins to wind down his complaints and climb back into the ambulance that had brought him to Fetterman, Minnie Coates bustled up, followed by two servants bearing blankets and pillows. The wife of Fort Fetterman's commanding officer took over for Sergeant Chandler, listening and shaking her head as the paymaster continued to bemoan his very existence.

While she was engaged, her servants entered the ambulance and quickly converted the horsehair seat into a tolerable bed. Sheets and blankets followed, and then a pillow, as the redoubtable Mrs. Coates edged Captain Perkins toward the vehicle. Before he even knew it, the paymaster was inside and the door closed.

"You just rest, Captain Perkins," the woman said. "You'll be at Fort Laramie before you know it."

She turned to Sergeant Chandler and made a washing motion with her hands as though she were Mrs. Pontius Pilate. "You get him out of here," she whispered to Hiram. "All he did was complain last night! Over dinner he informed me that anyone who would eat reconstituted apricots would probably drink his own bath water."

"He didn't, ma'am!" Hiram exclaimed in amazement. He had to turn away, hoping that the paymaster wasn't peering through some break in the canvas.

"He did, and right to my face! I thought Ed was going to choke on his string beans! The water was too alkaline, the bed too hard, our children too ill-mannered, the coyotes too noisy. You name it, he disliked it." She moved closer to the sergeant. "My husband told me to get rid of him. Just make sure I get the bedding back."

With that, she flounced back across the parade ground, followed by her servants.

"Give that lady a medal," Lieutenant Shaw said to the universe at large. "Now the big baby is ours. Sergeant, lead out."

Captain Perkins was theirs, but Mrs. Coates's influence continued to be felt throughout the day, as the little escort and the ambulance trailed beside the Platte River. When they halted for lunch and Hiram looked in the ambulance, he saw the paymaster clutching a half-empty bottle of Kentucky sipping whiskey that Lieutenant Shaw swore he had seen on the Coateses' sideboard.

"I have to hand it to the ladies," Shaw said as he quietly closed the ambulance door on the snoring, sodden mess within. "I wonder, Chandler, do you think Miss Hinchcliffe would handle such a matter so cleverly?"

Hiram thought Birdie O'Grady would, but he had his doubts about the lieutenant's light-o'-love, and hesitated.

"I rather doubt it too," Shaw said quietly, which gave the sergeant food for thought through the afternoon, as the escort moved along with all deliberate speed, even when June snow—the wet, heavy kind—began to fall.

Looking no better than probably ninety per-cent of Fort Fetterman's recently paid garrison, Captain Perkins emerged from the ambulance when they made a muddy evening camp along the Platte River. He blinked like a mole three years' underground, and retreated to the ambulance again, which the driver swore was beginning to stink of vomit and other unfortunate leavings.

"Just two more days," Hiram told him. "He'll be someone else's problem then. At least the snow has stopped."

Lieutenant Shaw glared at him, no more communicative than the paymaster.

I am surrounded by idiots, Hiram thought, and not for the first time. He spent the rest of the evening chatting with his corporal and privates, enjoying the soldiers he thought of as his. He had trained them, fought with them, and knew their value. He saw his own value in their eyes, and it warmed him as a fire never could.

The paymaster was destined to be their problem for longer than anticipated, which even gave

Sergeant Chandler—a man of duty—reason to pause and swear softly.

They were two hours into the next morning's travel when a courier rode up on a lathered horse. The courier, also from C Company, saluted smartly and handed Lieutenant Shaw a folded note. Shaw motioned Hiram closer so he could read the message too.

Hiram finished, gave himself a mental shake, and read it again, even as he saw his own dreams dribble away. Lieutenant Shaw turned a shade of red not found in nature and seemed to have trouble breathing.

"What do we do?" he managed to choke out finally.

"We follow orders," Sergeant Chandler said without hesitation, even though his heart hit rock bottom, somewhere down near his toenails.

There it was, spread out on Lieutenant Shaw's lap, a memo from Captain Coates, Commanding, that five idiots from A Company, infantry, had decided to take their greenbacks and five good horses and desert Fort Fetterman. A bunkie who hadn't gone along offered the information that these lame-brained pea shooters were going south through the Laramie Mountains to catch the westbound Union Pacific. Find them, clap them in the Fort Laramie guardhouse and get Captain Perkins on the Shy-Dead stage, then bring those lunatics back, the memo read.

This ruined everything, but the lieutenant resisted, to Hiram's discontent, but probably not his surprise. "We'll get Captain Perkins on the stage, then hunt for the deserters," Lieutenant Shaw said, louder than necessary, and pocketed the memo.

"Sir, with all respect, that's not what Captain Coates ordered," Hiram reminded his superior officer.

Thunder all over his face, the lieutenant jerked a thumb behind him and swung his horse around. Miserable, Hiram followed.

"If you think I'm going to show up too late to propose to Miss Hinchcliffe, you're sadly mistaken, Sergeant," Shaw hissed at him.

"It's an order, sir," Hiram stated.

This was precisely what Captain Harvey had warned him about, when C Company's captain left on furlough. *Guide him, sergeant. He might be a good officer someday,* sounded in Hiram's head as he stared down his superior officer, knowing that without rank, he had nothing behind him but the force of his own battle-earned experience and character. If Shaw commanded the escort to continue on to Fort Laramie, Hiram could lodge an official protest, but follow he must.

"We're discussing my future happiness," Shaw said, and Hiram let out a little of his held-back breath. Was his lieutenant weakening?

"Mine too, sir," Hiram said. He took a deep breath. "I was going to propose to Birdie O'Grady. I love her."

The two men stared at each other. For the first time, Hiram saw the potential in his lieutenant, a spoiled man from a wealthy family, who might, just might become the officer C Company deserved. It could go either way. Certainly the escort would grouse, but they would chase after five of their number who thought to escape the army. They would also follow their lieutenant's orders and go to Laramie first, if that was the decision. Hiram knew the troops had heard the first exchange between him and the lieutenant. He also knew that if Shaw disobeyed his commanding officer's order, the men would talk about it to other men. In a matter of days back at Fetterman, everyone would know they could not count on Lieutenant Shaw, not in small matters as this one probably was, and certainly not in larger matters of survival on a harsh frontier. Shaw would be finished, Hiram knew. Did Shaw know?

"Consider the men you lead, sir," Hiram said quietly. "That's all I ask."

Shaw turned his horse away. He stayed that way a long time. When he turned around, Hiram saw resignation, but also heretofore unseen resolution.

"Let's go find those miserable sinners, Sergeant," he said and they moved together toward the escort.

It took them two days, but they found four of the five miscreants, terrified now because one of their number had been killed by Lakota braves frisky after a winter on the reservation. They found them because Lieutenant Shaw had thought through the matter and gathered his little escort about him.

He showed them the memo, which impressed Hiram. "Gaither, O'Neal, Hales, Carter, and Wizner. Do any of you know these men?"

Fort Fetterman was a small garrison. Everyone knew the deserters as recent recruits from Eastern cities. "They don't know as much as we do about Indians and for sure not horses, sir," the corporal said. The other troopers laughed in that superior way of horsemen.

Hiram smiled to himself, pleased to know that C Company's veteran troopers had just included their Boston-bred lieutenant into the fraternity of battle-tried western soldiers, whether he knew it or not.

"What do you think they'll do?" Shaw asked the corporal, then included the privates in his question by looking around the little group.

Hiram knew. A glance at his corporal assured him that the men knew their sergeant knew too. They also seemed to understand what was at stake here in the education of an officer becoming fit to lead.

"They'll head for the Laramie Mountains, sure enough, sir," the corporal continued, as the troopers nodded. "That's the quickest way to the railroad."

"And the stupidest, sir," offered a private. Everyone laughed and the bond deepened.

"But they don't know horses and they don't know Indians," the corporal continued. "We'll track them easy enough and find them afoot, sir." His face grew serious. "If we're lucky, we'll find them before any reservation jumpers do."

And so they left the easy road to Fort Laramie and turned west and then south toward the mountains. Lieutenant Shaw took a moment to acquaint a more-sober Captain Perkins with the change of plans. He came back to Sergeant Chandler, plainly disgusted.

"That paymaster is a disgrace to the uniform, Sergeant," he said. Hiram gave a silent cheer to hear such a sentiment from the man he had almost been ready to discount as a disgrace, as well.

They made a dry camp that night and rose early in the morning, quiet and determined. An hour after sunrise, following Indian sign now, they heard gunfire to the south at the base of the mountains. It was short work to ride down a handful of hostiles biding their time taking occasional pot shots at four men in a buffalo wallow, most of their horses dead around them, and one of their number. Two Lakota went down under a few well-aimed carbines—C Company was noted for its marksmen—and the rest scattered, gone for good, or at least for now.

Captain Perkins had taken real exception to storing the dead man in his ambulance. Hiram quietly suggested to his lieutenant that they bury the man deep and leave a stone as a marker. Shaw agreed.

Perkins also objected to filling his personal ambulance with saddles from dead horses and two of the deserters, but Shaw ignored him. The remaining two deserters, hands tied together, sat on the one surviving horse. They were quiet, chastened, and relieved to be alive.

Fort Fetterman's escort of the paymaster arrived at Fort Laramie in the late afternoon of June 6. Swearing all manner of recriminations for abuse to his person and vowing lengthy letters to department headquarters in Omaha, and other luminaries higher up the chain of command, Captain Perkins took his leave. No one complained.

The deserters went to the guardhouse. A quiet word from Sergeant Chandler to the duty sergeant sent four other jailbirds under a guard to sluice out the ambulance. A few words with the guard led to a note for a laundress, who took away Mrs. Coates's soiled bedding to launder. Sergeant Chandler paid for her services out of his own pocket.

"Sergeant, care to walk with me to the Dunlaps?"

"Not certain I'm that brave, sir," Hiram said honestly.

"Well, walk a little ways with me," Lieutenant Shaw said, and it sounded more like an order.

They started across the parade ground to Officers Row, but the lieutenant stopped by the flagpole. Hiram looked around, suspecting that Shaw wanted to be out of hearing of the others. He braced himself for the tirade to come. He knew he had worked over the lieutenant and knew that other shoe was destined to drop.

Lieutenant Shaw looked down at his boots. When he raised his eyes to Hiram's, the sergeant saw something else, and took heart.

"I could have been really stupid two days ago," Shaw said. "Thanks to you, I wasn't."

Hiram made some motion with his hand, startled to hear Shaw's apology. "It's part of my job, sir." He chuckled. "Captain Harvey told me to keep an eye on you."

"He told me that too," Shaw continued, following his words with a rueful expression. "He told me, by gadfreys, to listen to my sergeant, because he knew more than I did." Shaw ducked his head again. "I'll confess that his words stung."

He looked up and Hiram saw the resolution he had noted so briefly, back down the trail. "I wanted to ignore you, but you wouldn't let me."

He held out his hand and Hiram shook it, surprised down to his socks, but more cheerful than he thought he would be, standing there staring at the Dunlap duplex over Shaw's shoulder and knowing Birdie O'Grady was gone for good.

Shaw grinned then, and he became the boyish, care-for-nobody fellow that Hiram knew even better. "When you write to Captain Harvey, tell him there's hope, will you? I mean, assuming that our captain wants a report from you now and then."

"Yes, sir, I will, sir," Hiram said.

Hands on hips, Shaw asked, "How many letters has that been so far?"

"Only one, sir," Hiram lied. "You're better than you think."

Shaw turned to look toward Officers Row. "I suppose I'll go find out just how much bad odor I am in at the Dunlaps. See to our escort, will you? I'm sure they'd like to bed down for a few hours."

"Yes, sir," Hiram said, thankful to have a task that took him away from what he suspected would be a fraught time for the lieutenant. Maybe the man really did love Miss Hinchcliffe, with her flighty, frivolous ways and unremarkable brainpan.

He found the C Company escort grooming their horses in the cavalry stable, and tidied up his own faithful remount, even though the men said they would do it. He noted with quiet pride that the men had already groomed and grained Lieutenant Shaw's horse, who was steadily munching through hay in a nearby loose box.

He sent the men to the cavalry barracks when they finished, where he knew they would find spare cots for a nap. He assured them he would join them soon. He was tired beyond belief and weary more in his heart because he wanted Birdie O'Grady as he had never wanted another woman in years. He was even more tired of duty, even though it had been the right thing, the honorable thing, the means of molding Lieutenant Shaw's character into someone who would be a leader eventually.

He dawdled his way toward the cavalry barracks, wanting to veer toward Officers Row, until he saw Lieutenant Shaw dawdling along too, head down, the portrait of rejection. Hiram waited by the sutler's store, willing to provide consolation, because that was what a good sergeant did, even as his own heart broke.

"Gone like the wild goose in winter," Shaw said, when they stood side by side. "Oof! Major Dunlap said his sister-in-law threw a fit worthy of royalty and flounced away on the Shy-Dead three days ago."

"I'm sorry, sir," Hiram said, and he meant it.

Shaw nodded. "I'll miss her." He laughed, and Hiram heard no sarcasm. It was a genuine laugh. "Major Dunlap said to me, 'Laddie, she wouldn't have fared well on the frontier. A woman has to be flexible.'"

"I'm sorry for you all the same," Hiram said, and still meant it.

"I am going to drown my sorrows in some single malt whiskey," Shaw said. "I think the sutler will open the officers' bar for me. Get some sleep, sergeant."

Hiram saluted and walked to the cavalry barracks. A sergeant in the stable had already told him to lie down on his cot in the barracks, so Hiram wasted not a minute in locating the room. With a sigh of profound gratitude, he closed the door behind him and flopped down on the iron bedstead. He sat up long enough to remove his boots and unbutton his trousers, then he dragged a blanket over him and promptly fell asleep.

He may have slept for hours, or maybe only minutes, when a knock on the door brought him awake immediately. He had no jurisdiction at Fort Laramie, but the person knocking wouldn't go away. He stood up and buttoned his trousers, but didn't bother with his boots. The soldier on the other side of the door would soon realize his mistake in sergeants and go away.

He opened the door on Birdie O'Grady. Her blushing face told him she had never been near a barracks before. Her obvious uncertainty suggested she wasn't convinced she should be here now.

Her look lasted only the bare second it took for him to gather her close in a tight embrace. Her hands came up under his arms and circled his back. He could feel her clasping her hands together, and knew she had no plans to ever let him go.

They stood that way a long moment until he pulled back so he could see her face. He kissed her for the first time, and knew right away it was going to be a kiss he repeated many times in the coming years. She seemed no more experienced in kissing than he was, but her hands went to his neck and into his hair. She pressed her lips into his with real intent, purpose, and ownership.

They each pulled away at the same moment. He suspected her look of wide-eyed disbelief at her spontaneous action mirrored his own.

She spoke first. "I thought you didn't want to see me, but I had to know for myself." She spoke the words so soft and low, her lips still nearly on his.

"What . . . what do you mean?" he asked, smelling rose talcum powder. He took a deeper breath and another until he caught the scent of Birdie herself underneath.

"Lieutenant Shaw didn't tell you I was still here?"

Hiram sucked in his breath, then started to laugh. He pulled Birdie into the room and closed the door, not wanting any chance spectators to see her there and speculate. He sat her down on the cavalry sergeant's bed. He sat beside her. Trust Lieutenant Shaw, in his self-centered misery, to forget a minor detail like Birdie O'Grady. The man might be on his way to success as a leader of men—all signs pointed that way now—but he had a ways to go yet. Shaw was still a work in progress.

"I think he was too bowled over by Miss Hinchcliffe's rejection to mention it," he said, willing to give Arthur Shaw the benefit of the doubt.

"I can imagine," Birdie said. "Glory be to all the saints, she threw quite a tantrum. And then when I stood there in front of her and resigned . . ."

Hiram took Birdie's hand in his and kissed it. "You did what?"

"I resigned. Dropped her flatter than a Shrove Tuesday pancake."

Hiram took it all in, relieved at the constancy of some women. "You hadn't heard from me in several months," he murmured into her hair, because she sat so close and he wanted her. "We learned later that the mail went astray."

She turned to him and kissed his forehead like a benediction. "I knew your heart, Hiram Chandler. I knew you would come for me."

"How did you find me here?" he asked, curious now, since his lieutenant had failed him.

"I went to the stable and inquired as to your whereabouts," she said, her face rosy again.

Or her face might have already been red from whisker burn. He hadn't shaved in several days. He sniffed himself, and knew he was currently no prize. "I need a bath," he told her, stating the obvious.

Birdie was a worthy match for him. She gave him that clear-eyed look again, which suggested she would keep him in line and love him more than he deserved. "You don't need a bath to propose to me, Sergeant Chandler," she said. "I'll take you as you are." She touched her forehead to his. "Major Dunlap says that is a very fine quality for women who follow the army."

What could he do except propose?

"Don't go down on one knee," his practical woman said. "That's silly and belongs in bad novels. Just ask me."

He asked and she said aye. He kissed her hand again, then walked her out of the barracks and onto the parade ground, his arm around her waist now because she fit just right.

"There's a vacant non-commissioned officer quarters at Fort Fetterman," he told her as they strolled along, generally heading in the direction of the admin building, where he knew Fort Laramie's chaplain could usually be found.

"Any furniture?"

"Not a stick," he told her cheerfully. "We can probably find some odds and ends in the quartermaster storehouse."

"I have sheets and blankets and one pillow," she said, leaning against his shoulder now.

"Same here. That's a start. Ammunition crates stack well and make good shelves."

They laughed about their lack of furniture and rugs and dishes and cutlery. Hiram couldn't think of a time in recent memory when he had ever felt happier about having few possessions. He glanced toward the sutler's store to see Lieutenant Shaw, leaning against the wall as though holding it up.

To Hiram's amusement, Shaw saw the two of them standing so close to each other and slapped his forehead, obviously remembering he had forgotten to deliver the whole message from the Dunlaps. He shrugged and went back inside.

"You'll like C Company," Hiram said as they cut across the corner of the parade ground closest to the admin building. "My captain is on furlough now, but he'll be back this summer. Lieutenant Shaw is learning. He'll be a leader of men yet."

"As good a leader as you?" she asked.

"Hard to say," he replied, so pleased with such a compliment from the woman who was going to be his wife by nightfall. "Ask me again in a few years, dear Birdie."

About the Author

Photo by Marie Bryner-Bowles, Bryner Photography

*T*HERE ARE MANY THINGS THAT Carla Kelly enjoys, but few of them are as rewarding as writing. From her short stories about the frontier army in 1977, she's been on a path that has turned her into a novelist, a ranger in the National Park Service, a newspaper writer, a contract historical researcher, a hospital/hospice PR writer, and an adjunct university professor.

Things might be simpler if she only liked to write one thing, but Carla, trained as a historian, has found historical fiction her way to explain many lives of the past.

An early interest in the Napoleonic Wars sparked the writing of Regency romances, the genre that she is perhaps best known for. "It was always the war, and not the romance, that interested me," she admits. Her agent suggested she put the two together, and she's been in demand, writing stories of people during that generation of war ending with the Battle of Waterloo in 1815.

Within the narrow confines of George IV's Regency, she's focused on the Royal Navy and the British Army, which fought Napoleon on land and sea. While most Regency romance writers emphasize lords and ladies, Carla prefers ordinary people. In fact, this has become her niche in the Regency world.

In 1983, Carla began her "novel" adventures with a story in the royal colony of New Mexico in 1680. She has recently returned to New Mexico with a series set in the eighteenth century. "I moved ahead a hundred years," she says. "That's progress, for a historian."

She has also found satisfaction in exploring another personal interest: LDS-themed novels, set in diverse times and places, from turn-of-the-century cattle ranching in Wyoming, to Mexico at war in 1912, to a coal camp in Carbon County.

Along the way, Carla has received two RITA Awards from Romance Writers of America for Best Regency of the Year; two Spurs from Western Writers of America for short stories; and three Whitney Awards from LDStorymakers, plus a Lifetime Achievement Award from Romantic Times. She is read in at least fourteen languages and writes for several publishers.

Carla and her husband, Martin, a retired professor of academic theater, live in Idaho Falls and are the parents of five children, plus grandchildren. You may contact her at www.carlakellyauthor.com or mrskellysnovels@gmail.com.

SCAN TO VISIT

WWW.CARLAKELLYAUTHOR.COM